DUCK AND COVER

Slocum cursed his luck. Another shot rang out. Another slug sent chips of rock flying. Slocum ducked low behind the rock. He glanced toward his big Appaloosa, longing for the Winchester hanging there useless at its side. He thought about making a run for it, but the shooter out there was a pretty damn good shot with his rifle. Still, he thought, a moving target is not as easy to hit as a still one. He waited. Another shot was fired at him. Slocum got back up into a low crouch and ran for the Appaloosa. The big horse fidgeted as Slocum came running at him, but Slocum got around to the animal's right side and grabbed the Winchester, pulling it free. He cranked a shell into the chamber as he ran back for the cover of the rock, and a shot shattered the ground just inches behind him.

He threw himself through the air, landing hard on his right shoulder and rolling over behind the rock. "Ah," he called out in pain. He scrambled up to a kneeling position behind the rock and took aim at the side of the hill where he thought the shooter was squirreled up. He fired. . . .

JAKE LOGAN

SLOCUM
AND THE
CIRCLE Z RIDERS

JOVE BOOKS, NEW YORK

SLOCUM AND THE CIRCLE Z RIDERS

A Jove Book / published by arrangement with the author

PRINTING HISTORY
Jove edition / July 2003

Copyright © 2003 by Penguin Group (USA) Inc.

For information address: The Berkley Publishing Group, a division of Penguin Group (USA) Inc., 375 Hudson Street, New York, New York 10014.

ISBN: 0-515-13576-3

A JOVE BOOK®
Jove Books are published by The Berkley Publishing Group, a division of Penguin Group (USA) Inc., 375 Hudson Street, New York, New York 10014. JOVE and the "J" design are trademarks belonging to Penguin Group (USA) Inc.

PRINTED IN THE UNITED STATES OF AMERICA

10 9 8 7 6 5 4 3 2 1

1

Slocum was pissed off. He'd had a bad day. That was for sure. As he walked into the Hognose Saloon, he called out for a bottle and glass. He tossed the last of his pocket change on the bar, took the bottle and glass, and moved to a vacant table by the far wall to sit down all alone and drink and sulk. By God, he was thoroughly pissed off. One of the saloon girls came over to his table smiling, but when she saw the look he gave her, she turned and hurried away. Standing at the bar with another of her kind, she whispered, and they both looked at him, scowling. Back at his table, Slocum poured himself a stiff drink of whiskey and tossed it down in one gulp. Then he poured another. He leaned back in his chair, his back to the wall, and considered the events of the last few miserable days.

He had been working at the Circle Z Ranch for old man Ziglinsky. Ziggie, as they called him, had hired Slocum to bust horses. He had just acquired a string of woolly ones. Slocum had been working for a month, and he had already made good riding stock out of a bunch of the critters. Then the hard rains came. Slocum just lay around the bunkhouse, or else he went into town for a few drinks. There was nothing he could do but wait out the hard weather.

Then came the day he was lying on his bunk, his boots off, his hands folded behind his head, his hat over his face, and he heard a hell of a commotion outside. He sat up on the edge of the bunk as three cowhands came running inside. They grabbed up some gear and headed out again.

"Hey," Slocum said. "What the hell's up?"

"Ziggie says we got to get over across Lizard Crick," one of the hands said. "We got some cows stranded over there, and the crick's rising. He wants them back over on this side right away."

"All hands out," said another of the cowboys. "Even you, bronc buster."

Slocum pulled on his boots and followed the others outside. He didn't mind a little hard work. It was better than being bored to death. He headed for the corral to get his horse and saddle it up, but just as he was approaching the corral, he saw Tobe, one of the old hands and a good buddy of Rance, the foreman, pulling viciously at the Appaloosa's reins. The big stallion was resisting. Tobe was cussing and threatening. Slocum hurried on over, put a hand on Tobe's shoulder, and spun him around. Tobe looked surprised as hell.

"Leave my horse alone," Slocum said.

"A horse is a horse," Tobe said. "We got work to be done."

He turned away from Slocum, still holding on to the reins. The Appaloosa reared and snorted. Slocum spun Tobe around again. Just as he was about to say something, Tobe let go of the reins and swung a hard right to Slocum's jaw. Slocum went over, landing on his back and sliding in the soft mud. The Appaloosa, free of Tobe's grasp, had backed away, still snorting. Slocum started to get up, but he slipped in the muck and fell again. Tobe laughed, and a couple of other boys joined in. Slocum finally got to his feet, rubbing his sore jaw.

"Hell," Tobe said, "take your damn horse. He ain't worth a shit anyhow. I'll get ole Blackie."

"Quit fooling around here," Rance said, riding up on his roan. "We got no time to waste. You boys ain't paid to roughhouse. Get a saddle on that damn horse and hurry it up."

Slocum burned with fury, but he kept quiet. He shook the mud off his hands as best he could, mounted his Appaloosa, and rode out of the corral behind Rance. He didn't like riding out the way he was, caked in mud and horse shit, but there was nothing to do about it but take it. The rest of the day was taken up in getting the cattle across Lizard Creek, and the job was done in the nick of time, although Slocum grumbled under his breath the whole time. The waters were running fast and rising high. Back at the corral at last, the sun about to disappear beyond the far horizon, Slocum unsaddled his big stallion and turned him loose in the corral. Tobe sniggered at him as he went past. Something inside of Slocum wanted to punch Tobe a good one, but his better judgment told him to hold his temper. He needed a bath and a change of clothes anyhow. He walked out of the corral and was headed for the bunkhouse when he heard someone call his name. He stopped and looked behind him. It was Rance.

"Come with me, Slocum," Rance said. "The boss wants to see you."

Slocum sloshed mud, trailing behind Rance and cursing to himself as they walked over to the big ranch house. Ziggie met them on the porch, looking stern. The rain had slowed down almost to a light drizzle, and besides that, the porch was covered. There were chairs on the porch, but old Ziggie was standing in his doorway, his arms folded across his chest. The stub of a cigar poked out of his tight lips underneath his ample white but stained mustache. Rance went up the stairs to stand beside Ziggie like a majordomo, but Slocum stopped at the bottom of the stairs, standing in the mud, the drizzle continuing to wet him down.

"What's this I hear about a fight in the corral?" Ziggie asked.

"It wasn't hardly a fight," Slocum said. "I never swung a punch. I just got knocked on my ass. That's all."

"How come?"

"There was a man abusing my horse," said Slocum. "I told

him to quit, and he didn't take kindly to my words. He hit me, but by the time I got up, he moved on to another horse. That's all there was to it. Ain't no harm done."

"Slocum," said Rance, "when a man hires on at the Circle Z, he hires on horse and all. Your horse is on the payroll same as you are, and when we're in a hurry to ride, a man grabs the first horse he comes to. Don't matter whose horse it is."

"No one said nothing about that to me when I hired on here," Slocum said. "Besides that, I was just hired to bust broncs. That's all."

"This was an emergency situation here," said Ziggie. "I needed every man out, and I—"

"I went," Slocum said. "And I never complained. I just got busted in the jaw is all. But no one ever said nothing about my horse working for you."

"But you provoked the fight, didn't you?" Ziggie said. "We'll let it pass this time, but you understand from here out that your horse is on my payroll right alongside you."

"No one rides my horse," Slocum said.

"Is that your last word on the subject?"

"It damn sure is."

"Then I'll get the pay you got coming to you. You can take your damn horse and ride on out tonight."

"Well, hell, that suits me just fine," Slocum said. "I was out of a job when I came here anyhow."

Ziggie turned and went inside the house. Rance looked down at Slocum, shaking his head.

"You're damn stubborn," he said.

"Hell," Slocum said, "ain't no one else can ride my horse anyhow. He's a one-man horse."

"Why didn't you say so to ole Ziggie?"

" 'Cause he didn't ask."

"Well, if you was to tell him, he might change his mind about firing you."

"I don't want the old son of a bitch to change his mind," Slocum said. "I'll be riding out soon as I get my damn money."

"It's getting kinda late, and you're all muddy," said Rance. "I'll get him to let you stay the night at least."

"Don't do me no favors," said Slocum.

"Well, hell. Suit yourself then. Stubborn bastard."

"First time I ever been fired on accounta being punched in the jaw."

Ziggie came back out. He handed Slocum's pay to Rance, and Rance walked to the edge of the porch and handed it down to Slocum. Slocum stuffed the money into a shirt pocket. As he turned to walk away, Tobe came sauntering up, looking cocky as hell. Slocum sure did want to knock the smirk off his shitty face.

"What's going on here?" Tobe asked.

"Slocum's leaving us," said Rance.

"He picked a good time, didn't he?" said Tobe. "Likely he planned it thisaway."

Slocum stopped and turned back to glare at Tobe.

"What the hell're you talking about?" he snapped.

"Hell, you been avoiding that mean, dirty, gray stallion out there like the plague," said Tobe. "You couldn't have put it off much longer. If you was to stay around, you'd a had to a-tried him right soon. I figger you're a-skeered of him, and that's how come you to start that trouble with me this evening. So you'd get your ass canned and wouldn't have to try to ride him."

"You son of a bitch," Slocum said. "You just come into town by yourself tomorrow. I'll be waiting, and I'll pound you into shit."

"Is he right, Slocum?" asked Ziggie.

Slocum turned sharply to look up at his former boss. "What?"

"Are you scared to ride that gray stallion?"

"Hell no."

"Then stick around till morning and show us."

"You just fired me."

"Tell you what," Ziggie said. "You stay the night, and in the morning, you try that gray bastard. If you ride him, I'll give you an extra month's pay."

"And if I don't?"

"I'll take back that what I just give you."

Slocum stared hard at Ziggie. "You're on," he said. He went back to the bunkhouse, got himself cleaned up, and went to bed in his bunk. Soon everyone on the ranch knew what had happened, and the other cowhands were asking him questions. Some were teasing him. He just ground his teeth and put his hat over his face. He'd show them in the morning, by God. He'd ride that gray horse, take that extra month's pay, and then ride out of this goddamned country for good. Damn Ziggie and Rance and Tobe. Damn them all.

In the morning, when Slocum walked to the corral, he found the whole crew, including old Ziggie, gathered up waiting for him. The gray stallion was all snubbed up to the post, saddled and ready for him. He stopped and looked around at all the grinning faces. Dropping his saddle roll to the ground, he ducked low and slipped through the corral fence rails without speaking to anyone. He stood for a moment and looked at the snuffling horse. Then he walked over beside it. He checked the saddle to make sure it was on right, checked the cinch strap. He studied it another moment, then swung up into the saddle. He set himself, pulled his hat down tight, and nodded his head.

"Let him go," he said.

The gray horse jumped straight up, and the crowd whooped and howled. When the critter came down, it landed hard on all fours at once, and Slocum felt all his guts jar. It kicked its hind legs, trying to dump him off forward over its neck. It fishtailed. It spun. It jumped straight up again. Slocum knew right away that he was in for a hell of a ride. The gray went to catbacking, pinwheeling, boiling over, swapping ends, and swallowing his head. Slocum felt himself jerked this way and that, tossed forward and then back. He was nearly unseated by a crawfishing move, and he grabbed leather for all he was worth. He could hear the roars from the cowhands on the fence. After some jackknifing, the horse started fence worming, and then all of a sudden, he kicked the lid off and Slocum along with it. Slocum went sailing. He flipped completely over in mid-flight, and he landed hard in a sitting position. It was a good thing that the ground was still soft with mud from the rain of the night before. The gray horse bucked straight away around the edge of the fence all the way around the corral twice. Then he kicked, stomped, snorted, and gave Slocum a hard look, his head down.

Slocum stood up with a moan and hobbled toward the fence, listening to roars of laughter, hoots, and jibes. He walked straight over to old Ziggie, reached into his shirt pocket, and handed back the month's pay he had received the night before. Then he turned to walk away without a word.

"Slocum," said Ziggie.

Slocum kept walking. He did not even bother looking back over his shoulder.

"You want your job back?"

Slocum ignored the old man and walked straight to his waiting horse. He mounted up and rode away without looking back. The catcalls and jibes and laughter followed him until he was far enough away that he could no longer hear them.

"Slocum, you can have your job back, if you want it," the old man cried, but Slocum was too far gone to hear what was said. He wouldn't have slowed down if he had heard it.

He rode away from the Circle Z with mud on the butt of his jeans and just a few dollars in his pockets. He rode away in a deep sulk. He no longer even wanted to punch out ole Tobe, because if he did that after all that had happened, well, it just wouldn't look right. It would look like he was a bad loser or something. He just wanted to get away from the Circle Z and get drunk. He figured he had about enough cash on him for a night in a hotel, a bottle of whiskey, and maybe a breakfast the following morning. He decided that he wouldn't even try to think beyond that. He headed for Rascality, the nearest town, and the Hognose Saloon, its best.

• • •

So there he sat in the Hognose trying to figure out what he had done wrong. Maybe he should have let his Appaloosa just kick and stomp the shit out of ole Tobe in the first place. But if the horse had killed Tobe, well, they might have insisted on killing the horse. Some people were funny that way. His brain was a little muddled from the drink, but he finally decided that he had done the only thing he could do. But then, maybe later on, when old Ziggie had offered him his job back, maybe he should ought to have swallowed his pride and accepted it. But thinking along those lines didn't make much sense either. He had his pride, by God. He was stuck with it, like it or not. There was no way he'd have taken that job back after all that had happened and all that had been said about him and about his horse.

Well then, what about stomping the shit out of ole Tobe? If he waited awhile before doing it, then it wouldn't look quite so bad. Maybe. But how long would he have to wait? He couldn't just lay around Rascality waiting, because he was about out of money, and he was for sure out of a job. He wondered if there might be any other jobs available in the vicinity. Maybe he would check around in the morning, after he woke up and sobered up. He poured himself another drink.

"I coulda rode that goddamned horse," he muttered out loud to himself. "Another try, I coulda done it."

He took a sip of the whiskey, and his back ached as he leaned back in the chair. He lowered the glass and groaned. It was about time he quit that damned job anyhow, he thought. The jouncing and jarring was tearing him up. A man could only take so many hours of being slapped around on the back of a bucking horse, so many times of being tossed through the air to land hard on the ground, so many rakes along the fence rails, so many kicks to his legs and butt and back. It was a hard way to make a few dollars, that was for sure. Still, he thought, he could have ridden the gray horse.

His hard look must have softened some, for one of the gals came back over to his table. She looked down at him with a soft, sympathetic expression and batted her painted eyelashes.

"You want some company?" she asked.

Slocum shrugged and gestured toward a chair. She pulled it out and sat down next to him. She was young, and she wasn't bad-looking. Slocum just wasn't in the mood. That was all. He didn't mind a little company though.

"I'm Rowdy," she said.

"I bet you are."

"No. That's my name. I mean, that's what they call me. Rowdy."

"Howdy," Slocum said.

"What's yours?"

"Whiskey?"

"That's your name?"

"Huh?"

"They call you Whiskey?"

"No. I'm Slocum. You want a drink?"

She looked toward the bartender and waved a hand. He got a glass and brought it over to her. Slocum poured it full. Then he refilled his own glass.

"Rowdy," he said.

"What?"

"Oh, nothing. I was just saying it. Rowdy."

"I can be too," she said. "If you like it that way. You want to get rowdy with me?"

"I ain't hardly fit for it tonight," Slocum said.

"You have a bad day?"

"It weren't one of my best. I can tell you that much for sure."

"You want to tell me about it?"

"Ain't much to tell. I got punched in the jaw. Lost my job and got throwed by a mean horse. I'm sore all over."

"I can fix that," Rowdy said.

Slocum looked at her and smiled for the first time.

"I bet you could," he said. "If I was up to it."

"Why don't we go upstairs?"

"Well, first of all, honey, I'm about drunk. Second, I got

just about enough money for a room. One without you. Then—"

"The room costs almost as much by itself as it does with me," Rowdy said. "The way the prices are, a man's a fool to buy a room without a girl in it. He's just throwing away his money. Let me see what you got."

Slocum dug the last of his money out of his pockets and tossed the bills on the table. He looked at her as she counted it.

"Hey, baby," she said. "You got it, and change to spare."

"Enough change for breakfast?"

"I'd say so. You wanta go upstairs with me now?"

Slocum lurched to his feet, grabbed the neck of his whiskey bottle in his left hand, picked up the glass in his right, and threw his right arm around Rowdy's shoulders to keep from losing his balance.

"Let's go," he said.

He wobbled some and leaned heavily on her as they made their way to the bottom of the stairs. Rowdy started to climb, but Slocum held her back. He tried to stand straight and still, but he was weaving. At last, he made the move. He put a foot on the bottom step and started up. Rowdy giggled a little.

"You all right?" she asked him. "You going to make it?"

"I'll make it," he said. "You just lead the way."

He noticed that his words were slurred. He was also aware, of course, of his weaving and staggering. He had not been drunk like that in a long time. But then, he had not been pissed off like that in a long time either. When they finally reached the landing, he rocked backward, and Rowdy put a hand on his back and pushed him ahead.

"I think you just saved my life," he said. "I'd likely a-broke my neck falling down them stairs." He turned around and looked back, checking out the distance he might have fallen.

"Come on over this way," Rowdy said, and she took him to a room, opened the door and went inside. She made their way across the room to the bed, and she dumped Slocum

unceremoniously on the soft mattress. Slocum moaned piti-
fully as Rowdy went back to close and lock the door. He
was staring at the ceiling as she moved back toward him. He
felt her pulling the boots off his feet, and he heard her, as if
at a distance, say, "I'm going to make you feel all better."
After that, he couldn't recall a thing.

2

Ole Ziggie closed with a slam the books he had been studying. There was something mighty damn wrong with the figures. The cow business seemed to be doing just fine, but the mine over on the far western edge of the ranch should have been showing a profit, and it was running in the red. Something was mighty wrong. Ziggie decided that he would ride over and pay a visit to the mine foreman, ole Charlie Dode. He wasn't quite ready to accuse Dode of stealing from him, but he meant to ask some hard questions. The figures in the book just didn't make any sense, and there had to be some explanation. Well, by God, he'd get it or else.

He walked over to the hat rack beside the front door, put his hat on, and walked out onto the porch. He headed for the corral where he spotted his ranch foreman. "Rance," he called out, "catch me up a horse. I mean to take me a ride over to the mine."

"Right away, Ziggie," said Rance. "But let me get someone to ride along with you."

"I don't need no nursemaid," the old man grumbled.

"Prob'ly not," said Rance, "but that's a long ride. In case of an accident or something, it's best to have someone along with you."

"Well, hurry it up then."

As Rance was throwing a saddle on a horse for his boss,

Tobe came riding into the corral. "You free, Tobe?" Rance asked.

"Yeah."

"Toss that saddle on a fresh horse then. Ziggie's riding over to the mine. I want you to ride along with him."

Slocum moaned and tried to open up his eyes, but they seemed to be glued shut. He rubbed them with the back of his hand and managed to open them to a squint. Slowly he remembered where he was, and just as slowly, he realized that for the first time in longer than he could remember, he was hungover. His head hurt. He thought about all the whiskey he had drunk the night before, and he decided that he was lucky he hadn't killed himself with the poison. He tried to sit up, and his entire body ached.

"Goddamn," he said. He wondered if it was the whiskey or the pounding the gray horse had given him. He rubbed his jaw, and he knew what had caused that. He got his feet on the floor, put his elbows on his knees and his head in his hands. At last he stood up and stretched himself. Then he walked over to the bowl of water on the table by the far wall. It seemed like a long walk. Leaning over, he dipped water in cupped hands and splashed it over his face. He felt around for the towel, picked it up, and rubbed the water off his face. Then he straightened up and looked in the mirror. He thought that he looked like hell. He knew he felt that way. A little breakfast might help. He felt in his pocket and found some change. Enough for some eggs and ham. And coffee. Lots of coffee.

He turned to leave the room. He was still fully dressed. All he had to do was pull on his boots, buckle on his Colt, and grab his hat. He stopped and hesitated, puzzled. There had been a girl. A saloon whore. Rowdy. He remembered it all then. She had helped him up the stairs. She must have pulled off his boots and unstrapped his gun belt. After that, she must have been disappointed. He must have passed right out. She hadn't even tried to get his shirt off. Oh, well, think-

ing back, he was pretty sure he had warned her of his condition, and besides that, it must have been obvious to anyone
who saw him that he wasn't fit for any serious cavorting, or
anything else serious for that matter. He finished getting
ready and went on downstairs.

Ziggie sat at a table in the mine office studying another set
of books. His face wore a deep frown. A stub of a cigar was
clenched between his teeth. He was thinking, among other
things, that he might just as well have been a goddamned
bookkeeper. Charlie Dode sat behind a desk watching nervously, and Tobe lounged against the wall off to Ziggie's
left and a bit behind him. Tobe looked at Dode, raising his
eyebrows. Then Ziggie slammed the big book shut and
looked up at Dode.

"Charlie," he said, "I know damn well more loads of ore
has gone out of here than what this shows, and I know damn
well there ought to be more money in the bank from it all.
What the hell's going on here?"

"I don't know what you mean, Ziggie," Dode said. "Everything's down right there. Exact. I keep good records. The
mine's playing out. That's all. It ain't producing what it used
to. You still got the old production schedule in your head,
but things have changed. It happens. Things change."

"Not that much," Ziggie said, "and not that fast."

"Damn it, Ziggie, you got the figures right there in front
of you. Figures don't lie."

"Sometimes the man who writes them down does," Ziggie
said.

Dode stood up fast. "Are you accusing me of stealing from
you? Is that it? By God, Ziggie, if that's what you're getting
at, then you look for some proof and go to the law. Swear
out a warrant and have me arrested. And you can find yourself another mine foreman while you're at it and see if anyone else can do a better job for you than what I've been
doing."

Ziggie got to his feet. "That's just what I mean to do,
Charlie," he said. "And if you hadn't just quit, I was going

to fire you. Pack up and get out. Tobe, come on. We're riding into town to see Burl."

As Ziggie turned sharply toward the door, Tobe and Dode exchanged surreptitious glances, and Tobe nodded. Then he followed Ziggie outside. At the bottom of the stairs, Ziggie and Tobe mounted up, turned their horses, and headed down toward the road.

"The son of a bitch is robbing me blind," Ziggie said. "I know it."

"But can you prove it, Boss?"

"I can get me a bookkeeper who can prove it," Ziggie said, "and I can find out where the ore has been sold and how much has been sold. If that don't match with Charlie's books, then I'll have him. If he knows what's good for him, when he clears out of here, he'll keep on riding before the law gets on his trail. He'll make his ass scarce around these parts, by God."

As Ziggie turned onto the road, Tobe fell a little behind. He slipped the six-gun out of its holster and thumbed back the hammer. Ziggie heard the telltale sound too late. He was turning his head to look back over his shoulder as the gun barked and jumped in Tobe's hand. The hot lead tore into Ziggie's back just between the shoulder blades, and blood spurted out through Ziggie's chest. The old man was dead in the saddle. His body sagged and slowly slid to one side to fall like a sack of grain down into the wet and sloshy muck of the road.

Casually, Tobe replaced the spent shell and reholstered his gun. Then he rode hard back to the ranch. As he was unsaddling his horse in the corral, Rance happened by. Stopping by the gate, the foreman asked, "Where's Ziggie?"

"Ah," said Tobe, "the old man's out there at that mine office pouring over them books. He told me to get my ass on back to work. He said he can't afford to be paying me to just stand around and watch him."

"Hell," Rance said, "that sounds like him all right. He's damn stubborn. I don't like him riding all the way back here alone though. He's getting too old to be acting like that."

"What could I do, Rance? He's the boss, and he told me to get."

"I know. I ain't blaming you. He's just stubborn is all. Maybe I'll find some excuse to ride out that direction here in a while."

"Everything okay, Boss?" asked a cowhand saddling up a horse in the corral.

"Yeah, Tex," said Rance. "It's just ole Ziggie grousing around again. That's all."

Slocum finished his breakfast and drank all the coffee he could hold. He was beginning to feel better. But he had very little cash left, and he was still dirty from the mud of the day before. He had not washed nor changed clothes since his bronc ride. He was conscious of people staring at him in the café and out on the street. He must look like a bum, he thought. He hated to think of using the last of his cash for a bath. He decided that the only other thing would be to ride out and find a secluded spot on the creek out of town. He had a change of clothes in his saddle roll. He decided that was what he would do.

At the edge of the creek, Slocum unsaddled the Appaloosa to let it drink and graze. He laid out his fresh clothes. He hung his gun belt on a branch near the edge of the creek, and then he stripped. Taking his muddy clothes with him, he waded into the water. He shivered as he squatted down to get his entire body under the water. He had just gotten used to the water temperature and was beginning to feel clean, when half a dozen mounted men rode up. He thought about reaching for his Colt, but quickly, he thought again. It was too late for that.

"Hey," he said, "can't a man get a bath in private around here?"

"Washing the blood off your hands?" said Rance.

Then Slocum noticed Rance for the first time, and he noticed that the man riding beside Rance had a badge pinned to his shirt.

"What's this all about?" Slocum asked.

"You know damn well," Rance said.

"Hold it, Rance," said the sheriff. "You John Slocum, are you?"

"That's me."

"I'm Burl Johnson. I'm the sheriff here. You have a fight with Ziggie yesterday morning?"

"We had words," Slocum said. "That's all."

"He fire you?"

"Yeah. Then he offered me my job back, and I turned him down."

"Well, someone shot him in the back this morning," Johnson said. "Killed him deader'n hell. Where were you at?"

"Killed Ziggie?"

"That's what I said."

"As if you didn't know," said Rance.

"I was in the hotel. I got up and had breakfast. Then I came out here. That's all. Hell, I didn't shoot Ziggie, the old fart."

"You don't expect the lying son of a bitch to admit it, do you?" Rance said. "An old man like that. Shot him in the back. And Slocum sitting there calling him names."

"I ain't a back shooter," Slocum said. "But the man never done me no favors."

"Both of you shut up," said Johnson. "Slocum, come on out of there and get dressed. You're coming into town with me."

"Am I under arrest?"

"Let's just say that you're under suspicion. Come on now. Hurry it up."

Slocum was humiliated. It had been the last straw. First he had been knocked down in the mud, then, trying to get to his feet, slipped in the mud and got laughed at. Then he had been thrown hard and laughed at again. He had been fired for nothing. He had been seen in town muddy and drunk, and he had spent the night in a hotel room with a pretty little whore and done absolutely nothing with her. Finally, he had been interrupted in his bath and arrested stark naked. Six men on horseback had watched as he walked gingerly out of the creek, naked and dripping, and pulled on his clean clothes still wet. Now he was sitting in a jail cell in Rascality accused of gunning an old man in the back. To top it all off, he had only about a dollar's worth of change in his jeans. He decided that if he ever got out of this damn jail, he would ride as far away from this damn country as he could get. Johnson walked over to the cell and poked a tin cup through the bars.

"Coffee?" he asked.

Slocum walked over and took the cup. "Thanks," he said, taking care not to look the sheriff in the face.

"You say you didn't do it?"

"That's what I say," said Slocum, "and it's the truth. Hell, I wouldn't kill a man over a job. And I sure wouldn't back shoot him."

"You didn't have nothing good to say about the old man," said the sheriff.

"I got nothing good to say about you either," Slocum said, "but I ain't planning to shoot you in the back. At least not yet I ain't."

"I checked over at the hotel and at the café," Johnson said. "They never saw you leave the hotel. You had a kind of late breakfast. They remembered you at the café all right."

"I was kind of conspicuous. All muddy from yesterday."

"But it was late enough that you could've rode out and shot old Ziggie and got back in time for your breakfast."

"But I didn't do it."

"Well, you've been accused. Likely there'll have to be a trial."

"Shit," said Slocum. "Damn it to hell, I was too drunk last night and too hungover this morning. I couldn't have rode off anywhere before breakfast."

"You got any witnesses who can prove that?"

"Hell no, I— Wait a minute. Rowdy."

"Rowdy? Over at the saloon?"

"Yeah. She might. She took me to the room last night. When I woke up this morning, she was gone. I don't know how long she'd been gone, but she may be able to give you some information that would help. I don't know."

Johnson nodded slowly. "Well, I'll go talk to her," he said. "I'll see you later. Don't go away."

"That's real funny, Sheriff," Slocum said, as Johnson headed for the front door. He sat on the edge of his cot to finish his coffee and consider his situation. It seemed that he had done everything wrong from the time he had caught Tobe trying to mount his Appaloosa. And now he was sitting helpless in jail. He wondered if he could break out somehow. If he waited for the right chance, he might. It could be the only reasonable thing for him to do. Unless Rowdy could prove that he had slept too long to have been able to ride out and kill old Ziggie, he was likely to hang. It wouldn't be the first time an innocent man had been hanged. He wasn't sure he could afford to wait around and find out.

He sipped the last of the coffee, put the cup down, and looked around the cell. If it had a weak spot, it wasn't visible. He stood up and walked to the window to test the bars. They were set tight. He walked around the walls and checked the door at the latch and the hinges. There was no way. He would have to wait for meal time and try to get the jump on Johnson. Without some outside help, that would be the only way. And he had no friends on the outside. It seemed to him, as a matter of fact, that everyone on the outside was ready to string him up. Slocum was thinking that ole Johnson had been gone for a long time, but when the sheriff came back in, he realized that it probably had not been all that long. Time seems to just drag along when you're sitting alone in a jail cell. As Johnson moved across the room toward his desk, Slocum stood up anxiously.

"She couldn't help much," Johnson said. "She was up and out of the room too early. About the only helpful thing she had to say was that she doubted you could've got out early enough to do the deed—drunk as you was the night before."

"That ain't much, is it?" Slocum asked.

" 'Fraid not," said Johnson.

It was as if the whole world had suddenly turned on Slocum. He was the one who had been done wrong, but far from getting any sympathy from anyone, he was sitting in jail, and it looked more and more like he was sitting there waiting to be tried for a sneaking murder. Damn, he thought, I should have just rode out here last night muddy and sober and damn near broke. I'd have been a whole lot better off and never known it.

Slocum's guts were growling by the time Johnson came in with a noon meal on a tray. On his way to the cell, the sheriff took the keys off a peg on the wall. He stepped on over to the cell and unlocked the door. Slocum stayed sitting on the edge of the cot so he wouldn't arouse any suspicion. Johnson took a couple of steps into the cell and leaned over to put the tray on the cot beside Slocum, and Slocum moved fast, almost without thinking.

He came up off the cot, flinging himself into Johnson's side and knocking him into the cell door. His momentum carried him along with Johnson, and he landed hard against the sheriff, and as Johnson's right hand went for the gun at his side, Slocum grabbed the sheriff's wrist. Holding the wrist with one hand, he grabbed a handful of hair with the other and banged Johnson's head against the bars. "Ahh," Johnson groaned. Slocum banged again and again until the sheriff went limp and slumped on the floor. Slocum checked to make sure he had not killed the man. Convinced that he had not, he took the gun from the sheriff's holster, and started to leave. He paused, had a second thought, went back for a biscuit, and then moved outside the cell, shut and locked the door, retrieved his own Colt, and hurried outside.

Out on the street, he walked casually, chewing on the biscuit. He did not want to draw attention to himself. He thought that he would be all right if only the sheriff stayed out cold long enough for him to find his horse. Likely it would be in the livery stable at the far end of the street. He walked that direction. Self-conscious, he felt as if all eyes were on him, but no one said anything. No one made a move toward him. If anyone said anything to him, he told himself, he would say that Johnson had gone to see Rowdy, then come back and turned him loose. He was anxious to put this damn town behind him, far behind.

He made it all the way to the livery stable and went inside. The man in there was sweeping the floor, and he looked up from his work at Slocum and registered surprise on his face.

"I've come for my horse," Slocum said.

"The Appaloosa?"

"That's right."

"You want me to saddle him up for you?"

Slocum could tell that the man was suspicious. And, of course, he would be. It must have been the sheriff who had left the horse there.

"Yeah," he said. "Go on."

The man laid aside his broom and went to a nearby stall. As he went inside, the big stallion snorted and fidgeted.

"Take it easy," Slocum said. "It's all right."

He'd have done the job himself, but he wanted to keep an eye on the stable man. The horse calmed at the sound of his voice, and soon he was saddled and ready to go. Slocum took the reins. He swung himself up and into the saddle. Then he reached into his shirt pocket for the change that was there.

"How much do I owe you?" he asked.

"Oh, nothing," the man said. "He wasn't here long enough to worry about it."

"Thanks," Slocum said, turning the Appaloosa toward the big stable door.

"Good luck to you," the man said nervously as Slocum rode out. Slocum fought back an urge to ride out of town fast and hard. Instead, he moved along at an easy pace, seemingly calm. He made his way out of town in that manner, and then he kicked his big horse into a run.

"Come on, big fella," he said. "Let's get the hell away from jerkwater son of a bitch."

He rode hard and fast for about a mile, and then he eased up again. He had been watching over his shoulder, and so far, he had seen no sign of pursuit. He was moving south along a well-traveled road. He considered that when they did figure things out and ride after him, they would come down that road. He decided to cut across open country heading west. There were some rolling hills off in the distance and some trees. If he hurried along, he would at least find some cover out there. He had already decided that if they came after him, he would not go back to jail without a fight.

It was dark by the time Slocum reached the first grove of trees, and he found a clear stream running by. He decided to stop for the night, wishing that he had some food with him. He did not though. He was lucky to have found water. He studied his back trail for a spell, and it seemed safe enough. He laid out his bedroll, but he built no fire. He had nothing to cook, and he did not want to draw anyone's attention. As he stretched himself out on the ground to try to get some sleep, he had a sudden thought that came to him in the form of a question.

What the hell am I doing? Why am I running? I didn't do anything, and I've made myself a fugitive. He thought hard for another moment before he made up his mind. He was going back. He was going to prove that he did not murder poor old Ziggie. In order to do that, he would almost for sure have to find out who did. Yes, by God, he was going to do the right thing. Then he thought again. He had banged that sheriff's head pretty damn hard, and the Circle Z foreman, ole Rance, sure did act like he wanted to see Slocum strung up and check out how heavy his ass might be. No. On second thought, maybe his first thought was the best. Just get as far away from Rascality and from the Circle Z as fast as he could.

3

Slocum had just gotten settled in for the night and was about to drift off to sleep when he heard the sound of approaching hoofs. He sat up quickly and slipped the Colt out of its holster. Then he waited. A damned posse? Already? No. There was only one horse. The horse came up nearer. He had to rely on the sound, for it was a dark night, and he was under the shadows of heavy trees. It couldn't be a pursuing posse, for it was just the one horse. He was sure of that by now. He supposed that a lone scout might have ridden out ahead of the rest of the posse. That was a possibility. But how the hell could anyone have tracked him right to this spot after dark? He wondered if he had been negligent in some way as he rode along. He thought that if anyone had been on his trail, he would have spotted him—or them. But someone was approaching. The hoofbeats drew nearer, then stopped.

Slocum heard the tired horse blow, and he heard from off to his right his own alert Appaloosa begin to fidget. Then in the night stillness, he could hear the creak of saddle leather as a rider dismounted. He could hear the feet hit the ground. Then slow footsteps came toward him. At last he could see a dark outline coming through the trees, and he thumbed back the hammer of the Colt.

"That's far enough," he said.

"Slocum?"

"Who the hell are you?"

"Myron."

"Myron?"

"You know. Myron Spraddler. From the Circle Z."

Slocum recalled the cowhand. A nice enough fellow. He had never had any problems with Spraddler, but then, they had never gotten that close either. "Are you riding with that goddamned posse?"

"No. Hell no. I come after you. I don't mean I come after you. Not like that. I come looking for you to have a talk. That's all."

Slocum considered for a moment. Then he answered, "What about?"

"I know they arrested you for killing ole Ziggie."

"They arrested me on suspicion," Slocum said. "That's all."

"Yeah," said Myron. "I know that, and I know that Rance is ready to hang you, but I also know that you never done it."

Slocum gave Myron a sideways look. "How could you know that?"

"Cause I seen it done, and it wasn't you that done it."

Slocum eased the hammer down on his Colt and holstered it. "Come on over, Myron," he said. "Did you see the posse coming out this direction?"

Myron walked through the darkness to where Slocum still sat on the ground. "Last I seen them," he said, "they was headed south on the road. Moving too fast to read any sign."

"Sit down," said Slocum.

Myron jerked a thumb over his shoulder. "I got some grub and some coffee in my gear," he said. "Want me to fetch it over? I know you lit out in a hurry."

Slocum thought about the meal he left on a tray in the jail. "That sounds good," he said. "I'll get a fire going."

As Myron walked back toward his horse, Slocum got up and began gathering sticks for a fire. "How's ole Johnson?" he asked. "Did I hurt him too much?"

"Give him a bump on the head and a headache is all," said Myron. "He sure does want to get his hands on you again though."

"Yeah. I bet he does."

In short order, Slocum had a fire going, and Myron had coffee boiling, beans heating, and bacon frying. He also produced some hard, ready-made biscuits. Slocum had some questions, but he figured they'd wait for the meal. Soon the two men had cleaned up all the victuals and poured themselves another cup of hot coffee. Slocum took a tentative sip.

"Myron," he said, "that sure is some better. I'm obliged to you. Now tell me, just what do you know about ole Ziggie's killing?"

"I was over by the corral whenever Rance told Tobe to ride out to the mine with Ziggie. I seen them ride out together. Well, a little later in the morning, I went out thataway myself. I wasn't going out there on accounta them. Hell, they wasn't even in my mind. I had some cow business out there. But I was up on a rise, and I seen Ziggie and Tobe a-coming back from the mine office. Ziggie didn't look none too happy. It was still and quiet out there, and I heard ole Ziggie say, 'The son of a bitch is robbing me blind.' That's just what he said. His voice carried out there real good. 'The son of a bitch is robbing me blind.' "

"Who was he talking about?"

"All I heard was just what I told you. That's all. But since they was coming from the mine, I figger he musta been talking about ole Charlie Dode, the mine boss. Anyhow, Tobe said something what I didn't catch, and Ziggie give him some answer, but I never heard that part too good neither, but while they was a-talking, Tobe let Ziggie ride a little ahead, you know, and of a sudden, he hauled out his six-gun and shot Ziggie right betwixt the shoulder blades. Well, I kept quiet as a mouse, on accounta I didn't want him a-coming after me. Well, then I was in town whenever they brought you in, and I heard how come, and I was a trying to figger out what to do whenever you busted out. I seen the posse ride south after a bit, and then I follered you. That's about it, I reckon."

"Damn it," said Slocum, "I wish you'd a-come into the jail before I knocked the sheriff's head against the bars."

"I reckon that woulda been better," said Myron, "but I was having myself a drink and thinking about what was best to do. I was thinking that if I was to say anything, why, I'd have Dode and Tobe after me, and I don't know who all else might be a-working with them. I ain't for sure about ole Burl Johnson. You know, I had to think it over some."

"Yeah," Slocum said. "I know. I ain't complaining. I appreciate you following me out here to tell me."

"I brung some whiskey too," Myron said. "You want some?"

"I sure do."

Myron got up and walked back over to his horse. In another few seconds, he was again seated at the fire. He uncorked a bottle and passed it to Slocum. Slocum poured himself a drink in the tin cup he had been using for coffee. Then he handed the bottle back to Myron. He waited until Myron had poured himself a drink and taken a sip before he tasted his own. It was good whiskey. But he thought about how drunk he had gotten back in Rascality, and he told himself that he did not want to allow that to happen again, especially with a posse on his trail, even if they were way off track.

"What're you going to do, Slocum?" asked Myron.

"I ain't sure," Slocum said. "I guess it partly depends on you."

"How's that?"

"Are you willing to tell Johnson what you just told me?"

"Yeah. Sure I am. You're right. I shoulda gone right in to see him soon as I knowed what was happening with you. But I've had plenty a time to think it over by now. I'll tell the sheriff ever'thing I seen."

"Then that's it. We'll just ride back in. You can tell Johnson what you saw and who did it, and that'll be that. I'll be free to ride on, and the rest'll be up to Johnson. It sure won't be our problem."

"When you want to head back for town?"

"Morning will be good enough," Slocum said. "The sheriff ain't likely back from his goose chase yet anyhow. Why don't you stay the rest of the night right here with me, and then we can ride back into Rascality first thing in the morning? All right?"

"Suits me," Myron said.

The next morning, they had breakfast, more coffee, cleaned up the camp, saddled their horses, and rode toward Rascality. Slocum felt good. He knew, of course, that if Johnson was a grudge holder, he just might make Slocum serve some time for escaping from jail by knocking him silly, but that was nothing, Slocum thought, to a murder charge. He would serve the however many days, then ride out a free man. He considered how amazing it was the way one's fortunes could change so much in such a short time. Last night, he had thought that he would spend the rest of his days a fugitive wanted for murder. Now, the worst he would have to face was short time for knocking a sheriff's head against the bars of his own jail. He chuckled at the thought.

"You meaning to ride on then," asked Myron, "once we get this here cleared up?"

"There's nothing to hold me around here," Slocum said. "What about you? You sticking with the Circle Z now that Ziggie's gone?"

"I reckon. I ain't got no other place to go. I reckon Marla will be for keeping me on. Marla and Rance. I been a pretty fair hand for them."

"Marla?"

"Yeah. That's ole Ziggie's daughter. That's right. You ain't never met her. She was off visiting relatives in the East whenever you first come around. She'll be coming back now. Matter of fact, I believe that she's coming into Rascality right away. With Ziggie gone, she's the boss, I reckon. 'Course, I imagine she'll leave the actual running a the ranch to ole Rance. He's been doing a pretty good job as foreman up till now. But she'll be the boss all right."

"There's no Mrs. Ziggie?"

"No. Poor ole Helen's been gone now for a couple a years. It's just Marla left now. That's all."

Johnson and his posse reached the small settlement of Roan Head, and after refreshing themselves and their horses, the sheriff asked a few questions. Then he called his posse back together. He had to get Tobe and a couple of other boys out of the saloon first.

"We been chasing the wrong rabbit, men," he said. "Slocum ain't been through here. He must've cut off the road back yonder somewhere."

"Which way?" a cowhand asked.

"The mountains west are rugged to cross," Johnson said. "My guess would be east."

"He might try them mountains."

"Yeah, he might," Johnson agreed. "I said it was a guess. I think I'll ride back for a few miles, then cut cross-country heading northeast. See if I can't pick up his trail. Are you all with me?"

"I'm with you," said Tobe. "The son of a bitch killed poor ole Ziggie."

"I'll stick with you, Burl," Rance said. "I want to get that back-shooting bastard."

The others all agreed, and Johnson said, "Let's ride."

"Anyone send a wire to the old man's daughter?" Slocum asked, as he rode easily along beside Myron.

"I been thinking on that," Myron said. "I don't reckon they did, on accounta I do believe that she was scheduled to come on back home today on the stage."

"Damn," Slocum said. "The poor thing will be coming home to bad news."

"Yeah. It won't be much of a homecoming for her, I reckon. Come to think of it, I don't even know who'll be there to meet her. Ole Rance rode out with the posse. I hope someone else remembers to meet the stage. I hate to think a her just a-standing around on the sidewalk all by her lonesome a-wondering how come her old man ain't waiting there for her. And him dead and buried."

"You think we could get back to Rascality before the stage rolls in?" Slocum asked.

"If we was to hurry along," Myron said, "I reckon we might could."

"Let's try it then. That way, if there's no one else there to meet her, you can do it."

They kicked up their mounts and loped ahead, but they had not gone a half a mile before they saw riders coming hard at them from the southwest.

"That there's the posse," Myron shouted.

Slocum slowed his Appaloosa and turned toward the riders. Myron followed his lead. They rode more slowly now, and they noticed that the posse also slowed its pace. Slocum took off his hat and waved it in the air. Myron did the same.

"Johnson," Slocum yelled, "is that you?"

Over with the posse, Tobe slipped the Winchester out of the saddle boot and cranked a shell into the chamber. Rance squinted.

"Is that Slocum?" he asked. "He's got someone with him."

"He's yelling something," said Johnson. "Let's move closer."

"It's him," said Tobe, and he raised his rifle to his shoulder, took quick aim, and squeezed the trigger.

"Ah." Myron jerked in the saddle and slumped. Astonished, Slocum reached over to check on Myron, but Myron, dead in the saddle, slipped off to one side and fell to the ground.

"Johnson," Slocum called. "Don't shoot. We got to talk."

Tobe's shot had infected other members of the posse though, and several rifles now barked, sending hot lead in Slocum's direction. Slocum lashed at the Appaloosa in a panic as he turned the big horse to race away to safety.

● ● ●

Johnson angrily knocked the rifle out of Tobe's hands and shouted to the rest of his posse. "Hold your fire, goddamn it. Hold your fire."

It took a while for his shouts to soak into the heads of the agitated riflemen. At last they stopped shooting.

"Damn you, Tobe," Johnson said. "What'd you do that for?"

"It was Slocum," said Tobe.

"It damn sure wasn't Slocum that you hit," Johnson said. "All of you, put those damn rifles away."

He rode forward to take a look at the victim of Tobe's hasty shot.

"Slocum's getting away," Tobe protested.

"Shut up," said Johnson. "I'm still in charge here."

"But Slocum's—"

"Shut up, Tobe," said Rance. "You heard Burl. I think you've done enough here anyhow."

Reaching the body of the fallen man, Johnson dismounted. The body was crumpled on one side, and Johnson straightened it out just as the others rode up.

"That's Myron," Rance said. "Is he—"

"Dead," said Johnson. "Tobe, there'll have to be a hearing on this."

"Hell," Tobe said, "if he was riding along with Slocum, then he musta been in on it with him."

"In on what?" Johnson said, exasperated. "Was he in on the fight Slocum had with Ziggie? Did Ziggie fire him too?"

"Well, no, but—"

"But nothing," Johnson said. "We weren't hunting Myron, and Myron wasn't wanted for anything. You killed him for nothing."

"He was with Slocum."

"Someone catch up Myron's horse," Johnson said. "Then load up the body. You're taking it back to Rascality."

"What about Slocum?" said Tobe.

"Tobe," said Johnson, "no one wants to get Slocum worse than I do. He busted outa my jail, and that makes me look bad. He also busted my head. But if I have to tell you one more time that I'm in charge here, I'll bust your head. It looks to me like you just killed an innocent man, and that don't seem to bother you at all. Rance, I want you to take Tobe here, and get on back to the Circle Z. I don't want to see him again on this trail. I don't want to see him when I get back to town. Just get him the hell out of my sight, but keep him in your sight. I'll want to see him at the hearing. I'll let you know when."

"Come on, Tobe," said Rance.

"But—"

"Shut up and come with me."

"The rest of you boys take this body and head back for town," Johnson said.

"What are you going to do?"

"Never mind that. That's none of your damn business. This posse is officially disbanded. Just do what I say. Get going, damn it."

Johnson stood watching until the last grumbling rider was a small dot on the far horizon. Then he climbed back into the saddle. He didn't know who he was maddest at, Slocum or Tobe. It was curious to find Myron riding along with Slocum, but that sure didn't make Myron guilty of anything, and it would have been much more productive to hear what Myron and Slocum might have had to say. They had actually been riding toward the posse, and neither one had pulled a gun. Johnson thought that it was a good thing he had sent Tobe away with Rance, for he sure did feel like pounding the shit out of the surly cowhand.

And about Slocum—there did seem to be some doubt about his guilt. Then the son of a bitch had jumped Johnson in his cell, pounded his head against the bars, and escaped, so guilty or innocent of murder, Slocum had damn sure pissed off Johnson. But Johnson had not wanted to start shooting first without having asked some questions. He urged his horse forward, following the trail of Slocum. Maybe Slocum would still want to talk. Johnson doubted it though. Not after he had been fired on without provocation. He knew that Slocum had a good head start on him, having taken off at a run on that big, powerful stallion of his, but he also knew that Slocum could not run even that horse forever. He would have to slow down and rest some time. He plodded steadfastly along on the trail. Damn it. His head still hurt.

In Rascality, Rance saw the stagecoach pulling into town, and he remembered that Ziggie had been planning to meet Marla. When Ziggie had been murdered, Rance had forgotten all about the stage. He was glad that he had gotten back into town in time, but he was not looking forward to being the one to have to tell her about her father.

"Tobe," he said, "ride on back to the ranch. I'll be along in a while."

"I think I'll just go in the saloon and wet my whistle," Tobe said.

"I said get back to the ranch," said Rance, "and I meant it. You stay in town another minute, and you're fired. Well, what's it going to be?"

Tobe ground his teeth together in anger, but he turned his horse quickly and rode hard out of town in the direction of the Circle Z. Rance rode to the nearest hitch rail, dismounted, and tied his horse. He heaved a heavy sigh, snugged his hat down, hitched his britches, and walked toward the stagecoach, which was still rocking back and forth after its sudden stop.

4

Charlie Dode was working over some ledgers at his desk in the mine office when he heard the sound of a rapidly approaching horse. He jumped up and strode over to the window to look down on the road that led up to the mine. He could see the horse and rider but not clearly enough to recognize them.

"Chance," he shouted out the window.

Down below a burly unshaven man looked up toward Dode.

"Yeah?"

"Who's that coming?"

Chance looked toward the rider, shielding his eyes against the glare of the sun. Then he turned toward Dode again. "It's Tobe," he called out.

Dode sighed with relief and went back to the chair behind his desk. Ziggie's suspicions had rattled him, and then he'd had Ziggie murdered. His nerves were a bit raw. He was on edge. There was always the possibility that someone other than Ziggie was also suspicious. Ziggie might even have confided in someone. And then too, perhaps Tobe hadn't covered up the killing well enough. Dode was wrestling with the thought of pulling out, getting out while the getting was good, but then, he considered, it might look bad for him if he were to pull out right after Ziggie's murder.

That's what he was working on. He was trying to figure out just how much he could get away with, just how he should pull it off, and how soon it would be safe to make his move. And not just that. How late would be too late? They were all big questions, and Charlie Dode wanted to answer them just right. He wanted no slipups, and if there were any, he did not want them to be his own. He looked up from his work when Tobe walked in.

Tobe jerked the hat off his head and slapped it down onto a tabletop. He stomped over to a cabinet and took out a bottle and a glass, poured himself a healthy drink of whiskey, then sat down at the table. Dode watched as Tobe took a long swallow.

"Something eating you?" he asked.

"Ah, that damn foreman."

"Rance?"

"Yeah. That son of a bitch."

"I thought you was getting along real well with ole Rance," said Dode. "What's the problem?"

"Well, that stupid fucking Johnson let Slocum bust outa jail," Tobe said, "and so he called a posse. I went with it, so did Rance. We run Slocum down all right, and there was someone else with him. Well, I went to shooting and dropped the other feller, and I coulda dropped Slocum too, but Johnson and Rance stopped me. The posse broke up. Johnson kept after Slocum all on his own, I guess, and me and Rance rode back into town. I was heading for the saloon, but Rance told me to get my ass back out to the ranch. He ain't got no call talking to me like that."

"Who was it you killed?"

"What?"

"The man with Slocum that you killed—who was he?"

"Oh, him. It was that cowhand Myron, that's all." Tobe finished his drink and got up to walk back to the cabinet to refill his glass. "Hell damn, if they hadn't a-stopped me, I'd a killed that damn Slocum too, and that'd be the end of it. Ever'one thinks he killed Ziggie, and with him dead, there wouldn't be no one to even deny it. Case closed."

"I see what you mean," said Dode.

"It woulda been slicker'n owl shit."

"Yeah. Well, at least Slocum is still under suspicion, and now that he's broken out of jail, and he's on the run, that makes him look even more suspicious. I'd say at least no one's looking in our direction."

"What if Johnson brings him back alive? Huh? What if there's a trial? What then? There'll be a lot of talk, lots a questions being asked. If Slocum gets him a good, smart-ass lawyer, they'll be looking in ever' which direction. Won't they?"

"You're right about that," said Dode. "Say. You think you could ride after Johnson and catch up?"

"He done sent me off."

"But could you?"

"I reckon I could. How come?"

"I was just thinking. What would people think if Sheriff Johnson was riding after Slocum all alone, and he came up dead? Shot out on the trail."

Tobe turned down his glass and drained it. He looked over at Dode with a glimmer in his eye. "What could they think?" he said. "A course, they'd think that Slocum done it."

Rance waited until he had driven Marla back to the ranch and unloaded her luggage into the ranch house before telling her the bad news. It just didn't seem right to tell her in town nor out on the road. Besides, he was putting it off as long as he could. He knew that. But once she was actually in the big house, there was no more putting it off. She was looking for her father. She had to be told, and so he told her. She had a brief cry, and then she became angry. Rance was thinking that she was ole Ziggie's kid all right. No time for sentiment. All business and tough as nails.

"Who did it, Rance?" she demanded.

"Everyone thinks it was done by a man name of Slocum," said Rance. "He was working here as a bronc buster. Pretty good hand. But ole Ziggie fired him. Slocum left out of here in a kind of foul mood. Burl arrested him, but he busted out of jail. Burl's out trailing him right now."

Marla felt as if she had at once been told too much and too little. "Wait a minute, Rance," she said. "Did anyone see the shooting?"

"No, ma'am," Rance said. "No one that we know of."

"So you accused this Slocum because Dad fired him? Is that right?"

"Well—"

"That's not much evidence, is it?"

"Well, no, I guess it ain't, but once he was arrested, he did bust out of jail and run."

"What would you do if you thought you might hang for something you didn't do?"

"I reckon I'd run like hell."

"Exactly. Let's go back to the beginning. Why did Dad fire Slocum?"

Rance told the whole tale, starting with the fuss in the corral over Slocum's horse and Slocum getting knocked down in the mud by Tobe. He wound it all up with Slocum's attempt at riding the gray stallion, and Ziggie offering him his job back. "But Slocum never even answered him. He just stomped off, got on his horse, and rode away."

"Why would Slocum kill Dad for firing him if Dad offered him his job back?" Marla asked.

"Well, he was mighty riled up over the whole business," said Rance.

"Yeah," she said. "Maybe. So Slocum rode off. When was Dad shot?"

"It was the next morning. He had rode out to the mine office, and he was shot on the road on his way back here."

"No witnesses?"

"None."

"So how come Slocum got arrested?"

"Well, I reckon I brought that about," Rance said. "When I reported the killing to Burl Johnson, I told him all about the firing and all. We went and found Slocum. Burl questioned him and took him in."

"Rance, if Slocum killed my father, I want to see him hang as much as anyone. More. But I don't want to see just anyone hang for this. I want to know that I'm seeing the right one hang. I want to know that we got the right man."

"Yes, ma'am."

"What do you know about Slocum?"

"I heard some talk that he's some kind of a gunfighter. Just talk. I don't know."

Marla paced the floor in deep thought. "Rance, if you were a gunfighter, and you thought someone had done you dirty, would you shoot him in the back, or would you face him so he'd know who was fixing to kill him and why?"

"I reckon I'd face him all right."

"How did Slocum break out of jail?"

"Best I understand it," Rance said, "Burl went into the cell to give him his lunch, and Slocum jumped him. Banged his head on the bars and run off."

"He didn't shoot him?"

"No."

"You said that Burl's riding after him right now. Alone?"

"Yes."

"No posse?"

"Well, we did have a posse, but whenever Tobe killed Myron, Burl got all hot and run us all off."

"Whoa," said Marla. "Tobe killed Myron? Are you talking about Myron Spraddler?"

"Yes, ma'am." Rance then had to tell the whole tale of what had happened with the posse and why he and Tobe were no longer out there with the sheriff on Slocum's trail.

"I want to know more about Slocum," Marla said. "He sounds to me like he's either no gunfighter, or he's no cold-blooded killer. He didn't fire back at the posse?"

"No, he never."

"Rance, I'm going to change my clothes. You saddle us a couple of horses. We're going back into town. We have to get to the bottom of this."

•   •   •

Slocum had ridden the Appaloosa as long and as hard as he dared. He could see the rider coming after him, and he wondered what had become of the rest of the posse. He figured his big stallion could outrun the best of them, but after all, there was only one man. Why abuse the horse? Rolling hills were just ahead, and he made straight for them. Soon he spotted a little valley that looked as if it had been used as a trail before. He made for it. As he rode into the valley, the sky seemed to darken. He slowed his pace and looked for a possible side trail. In a short while, one appeared. He took it, and found a place to hide the Appaloosa. He dismounted, took his rifle, and scurried up the hillside, locating a spot he could hunker down in and have a view and a straight shot at the trail below. He cranked a shell into the chamber of the Winchester and settled down to wait.

Burl Johnson stopped at the entrance to the dark valley. He guessed what Slocum was up to. No man in his right sense would run his horse to death out in the wild like this. With a layout like this valley, he would ride in and lay an ambush. Johnson looked right and left, but he could find no other way into the hills, no way of maybe slipping around and up behind his prey. The only thing was to ride into the valley, to ride right into the ambush that he knew would be waiting for him. Either that or turn around and go back empty-handed. He didn't want to do that. He had never run away from a fight before. He had never abandoned pursuit of a fugitive.

But he was not feeling suicidal either. Maybe, he thought, if he rode slowly and kept to one side of the trail, he could watch carefully for any ambush sites and then keep close to the same side of the trail as the possible spot. That would make a down shot more difficult. He might be able to talk Slocum down. If not, he might at least have a fighting chance. But in spite of Slocum's surprise attack in the jail, Johnson did not think that Slocum was a skulking murderer or a coward. He believed that Slocum would give a man a chance. He decided to gamble his life on his belief, and he urged his horse forward.

Slocum recognized Burl Johnson down below on the trail. Again he wondered what had become of the rest of the posse. Could it be some kind of trick? He couldn't think what the trick would be, but he did wonder why a sheriff with a posse on a fugitive's trail would go on ahead alone. It couldn't have taken the whole posse to lug poor ole Myron back to town. He waited until Johnson had ridden past him.

"Hold it right there, Sheriff," he called out.

Johnson halted his mount and held his hands up.

"You told me you're not a back shooter," he said.

"Then the safest thing for you is to not turn around," Slocum said. "Just sit still the way you are right now."

"I'm not moving."

"Where's your posse?"

"I sent them back," Johnson said. "They were too trigger-happy."

"I'd say so. Why don't you slip that six-gun out real easy and drop it?"

Johnson did as Slocum said.

"Now the rifle," said Slocum.

Johnson dropped that, and Slocum made his way down the hillside to stand behind Johnson. He picked up the two guns and tossed them out of Johnson's reach. "You can come on down and turn around now," he said.

Johnson climbed down and turned to face Slocum. "How come you knocked the shit out of me back in my jail?" he said.

"I thought it would be smart of me to get the hell out of there. Everyone seemed to have me guilty and ready to hang."

"You say you didn't do it?"

"I didn't do it. Hell, if I was a back shooter, you'd be a dead man right now."

"I'm inclined to believe that," Johnson said. "But Slocum,

you have to go back with me and stand trial. That's the only way to clear your name."

"It's the only way to get my neck stretched too," said Slocum.

"What was Myron doing out here with you?"

"Is he dead?"

"He's dead."

"Goddamn it. The poor bastard. Well, then there ain't much sense in me telling you what he was doing out here. How come you to kill him like that? He didn't do anything."

"I didn't," Johnson said. "I told you, that bunch was trigger-happy. When Tobe just shot without warning and without waiting for my say-so, I sent them all back. I'm sorry about Myron."

"Tobe, huh? I'm not surprised. He's an asshole. Sit down, Sheriff."

Johnson looked around and picked out a spot at the base of a hill behind him. He sat. Slocum walked over and sat beside him but a few feet away. "Sheriff," he said, "I bedded down last night, and Myron slipped up on me in my camp. Embarrassed the hell out of me. I thought I was better at covering my trail than that. Anyhow, he told me that he came after me deliberate-like, because he knew that I hadn't killed Ziggie. He saw the killing. He was going to ride back into town with me to tell you what he saw."

"You say he witnessed the killing?"

"That's what he told me."

"Did he say who did it?"

"Yep."

"Well, who was it?"

"It was your buddy Tobe."

"Goddamn," said Johnson.

"Now Myron's dead," said Slocum, "you got nothing but my word for what he said. I'm right back where I was before."

"I'm not so sure about that, Slocum," Johnson said. "I'm not sure why, but I believe you. Did Myron say anything else about what happened?"

"He said that Tobe and Ziggie rode out together. They went over to the mine office. Tobe shot him in the back on the return trip. The only thing he heard was Ziggie saying something like, 'The bastard's robbing me blind.' That's all."

"Slocum," said Johnson, "ride back with me. You won't be under arrest. All I had you for anyway was questioning. We'll forget that little matter of a jailbreak and assaulting an officer. I'll bring Tobe in for questioning."

"That's what you took me in for. How far you going to get with that?"

"We've got a little more to go on now."

"Not without Myron."

"Someone else is bound to know that Tobe was riding with Ziggie. That makes Tobe the last man to see him alive, and that makes him a prime suspect. We can start with that."

Slocum rubbed his chin in thought. "Yeah," he said. "It's kind of interesting too that he's the one that shot poor Myron. The only witness. Although Myron didn't think he'd been seen."

"Will you go back with me?"

"I'm thinking on it," Slocum said. "You got any coffee with you?"

"I do. Got some grub too."

"Let's make a little camp for the night. I'll answer your question in the morning."

"Fair enough."

"Did you mean it when you said I ain't under arrest no more?"

"I meant it."

"You can pick up your guns then," Slocum said. "I'll get us a fire started."

Marla walked boldly into Burl Johnson's office followed by a sheepish Rance. She moved around behind the big desk and immediately began rummaging through papers there on top. "Marla," said Rance.

"What?"

"Well, you can't just go through those papers like that."

"Why not?" she said, and she sat down and started opening desk drawers. "Burl's not here to ask permission of."

"Well, what're you looking for?"

"Anything about John Slocum," she said. In another few minutes, she stood up, disappointed, and she headed for the door. "Come on," she said.

"Where to now?"

"The telegraph office," she said.

Slocum and Johnson were up early the next morning. Slocum got the fire going again, and Johnson put on some coffee to boil. Slocum was again pondering the fast changes in his fortune. Just yesterday, he had been a hunted fugitive, wanted for murder, a likely suspect for a necktie party. Now here he was having morning coffee with the sheriff. They were acting like ole pards. He reached into his shirt pocket for a cigar, and he discovered that he had two left.

"Have a smoke with me while the coffee boils?" he asked, holding one out toward Johnson.

"Sure," said Johnson. "Thanks."

As he reached out his hand for the proffered smoke, a rifle shot resounded, echoing through the valley. Johnson jerked and fell forward. Slocum caught him and kept him from falling on his face, but he hoped that it mattered. He hoped that he was not catching a corpse.

5

He hoped that he was not catching a corpse, but he didn't have time to find out. He lowered the limp body down to the earth as easily as he could, still hurrying and looking wildly around at the same time. Someone was out there with a rifle, and the next shot would likely be aimed at him. Pulling his arms from under the weight of the sheriff, he crouched and ran, just as another shot kicked up dust right behind him. He made a dive for a hidey-hole at the edge of the trail.

Another shot rang out, and the lead pinged against the large rock behind which Slocum crouched. This time he thought that he could tell where the shot came from. It was about as far away as a man could be and still get off a good shot with a rifle. Slocum's rifle was in the scabbard tied onto his saddle. There was no way he could get to it. He didn't even bother pulling out his Colt. It would be totally useless at that range. All he could do was stay snugged down behind the rock and wait the ambusher out.

That would not ordinarily be a problem. He could be long on patience. The problem was Sheriff Burl Johnson. If he was lucky enough to still be alive, he would need attention fast. Slocum couldn't tell if there was any life left in the sheriff's body. He thought of the quick changes in his fortune again. The rapid ups and downs. Here he had been a wanted fugitive suspected of murder. Then a witness had appeared, almost out of nowhere to clear him, but the witness had been murdered. Even so, when the sheriff had come upon him, he had believed Slocum's story. Then with the sheriff on his side, Slocum had begun to relax. Now the sheriff was lying on the ground with a rifle slug in his back, dead or nearly so, and the culprit was still out there pinging away at a helplessly pinned down Slocum.

Slocum cursed his luck. Another shot rang out. Another slug sent chips of rock flying. Slocum ducked low behind the rock. He glanced toward his big Appaloosa, longing for the Winchester hanging there useless at its side. He thought about making a run for it, but the shooter out there was a pretty damn good shot with his rifle. Still, he thought, a moving target is not as easy to hit as a still one. He waited. Another shot was fired at him. Slocum got back up into a low crouch and ran for the Appaloosa. The big horse fidgeted as Slocum came running at him, but Slocum got around to the animal's right side and grabbed the Winchester, pulling it free. He cranked a shell into the chamber as he ran back for the cover of the rock, and a shot shattered the ground just inches behind him.

He threw himself through the air, landing hard on his right shoulder and rolling over behind the rock. "Ah," he called out with pain. He scrambled up to a kneeling position behind the rock and took aim at the side of the hill where he thought the shooter was squirreled up. He fired. He cranked the lever and fired again. He waited, but no shot was returned. At last he heard the sound of hoofbeats, and then he saw the horse and rider appear in the distance hurrying away. The man was a coward. A back shooter who turned to run when someone fired in return. He couldn't have sworn to it in a court of law, but he was sure that the shooter had been Tobe.

For an instant, Slocum considered jumping onto the Appaloosa and racing after Tobe, or whoever it was, but then he shot a glance over at the seemingly lifeless body of Sheriff Burl Johnson. He hurried over to kneel beside Johnson and make a closer inspection. He was astonished to discover that there was still life in there. It was a long way back to town though, and it would be a rough ride for a man with a hole in his back. Slocum went to work on the wound, patching it up as best he could. Then he caught up Johnson's horse and loaded the sheriff onto the saddle like a sack of grain. It wasn't the best way for the poor son of a bitch to travel, but it was the best that he could do at the time. Holding the reins to Johnson's horse, Slocum mounted his Appaloosa and started to ride. Along the way, he realized that it would be shorter and quicker to ride to the Circle Z Ranch. He hoped that he could take Johnson up to the ranch house without getting himself shot on the way in. He tried to think of some other way to take care of the problem, but nothing more came to him. He kept riding.

Tobe whipped his horse into a lather and himself into a frenzy. He thought about riding straight into Rascality and the Hognose Saloon for a drink, but then he recalled that Charlie Dode kept whiskey at the mine office, and he felt that he would be somehow safer out there. He decided to ride for the mine office. Damn that Slocum, he thought. He had come so close. If only he had been a little faster with his second shot, he would have gotten both the sheriff and Slocum, and his problems would all have been solved. At least, he thought, Slocum was now absolutely alone. There was no one left on his side. Everyone was convinced that Slocum had murdered poor old Ziggie in cold blood, and almost everyone would be ready to shoot Slocum on sight. That was better than nothing.

At the Circle Z, Marla sat in the ranch house behind her father's big desk. She was looking through a small stack of papers when the front door opened a crack and Rance peeked in. "Miss Marla?" She looked up.

"Come on in, Rance," she said.

"You want to see me, ma'am?" Rance asked, as he moved into the big room.

"Come on over and have a chair," Marla said. "I've been

reading the answers to those wires I sent out inquiring about John Slocum."

"Yeah?"

"They're a bit confusing," she said. "Everyone seems to agree on one thing. He's a gunfighter all right. And a damn good one, it seems."

"I thought so," said Rance.

"But some of the comments praise him highly."

"There are them out there who admire killers, miss."

"No. Listen to this. 'Slocum is one of the best shootists around. No question. But if you're looking to hire yourself a gun, you best look elsewhere. He don't like hiring out thataway. Now and then, if he's sure he's on the right side, he'll do it.' "

She put the paper down and looked at Rance waiting for some kind of response. When she got none, she said, "Well?"

"Well, I don't know," Rance said with a shrug. "That don't sound like no back shooter."

"No," she said, "it doesn't."

"Miss Marla," said Rance, "I'm coming to think like you. There's something mighty wrong here. If Slocum's like what that there wire says, he wouldn't have shot Ziggie in the back like that. And, yeah, he did bonk Burl's head and all and bust outa jail, but then, we all was dead set that he was the killer. Could be, he seen that as the only sensible thing to do. Then whenever we come on him and poor ole Myron out there, him and Myron come a riding at us, and they didn't draw no guns. Tobe went and shot first, killing Myron. Slocum didn't run till then."

"I don't believe that Slocum is our man," Marla said. "Still, I would sure like to have a talk with him."

"Well, maybe ole Burl'll bring him back in."

"Maybe."

"Uh, Miss Marla, you want me to take some of the boys and ride out looking for him?"

"The sheriff sent you back once already," she answered.

"Well, we'd sure enough have us a different attitude if we

was to go out again," Rance said, "and I sure wouldn't take Tobe along again."

"It seems hopeless," Marla said. "I mean, Slocum's had plenty of time to get well away from here, hasn't he?"

"Unless Burl's caught up with him or slowed him down some way."

"Maybe we should just wait for the sheriff," she said. "In the meantime, we can try to figure out some other angle. If Daddy wasn't killed by a disgruntled cowhand he had just fired, then who and why?"

"Everyone loved Ziggie," Rance said.

"Not everyone, Rance. Someone shot him in the back and killed him."

"I can't think who would do a thing like that."

"You said Daddy was coming back from the mine when he was killed. Right?"

"That's right."

"And you had sent someone to ride along with him?"

"Yeah. I sent Tobe."

"So where was Tobe when it happened?"

"Tobe come back earlier. He said that Ziggie had told him to come on back. Said he didn't need him. That makes sense. Why, whenever I sent Tobe along in the first place, Ziggie growled at me that he didn't need no nursemaid."

Marla stroked her chin. "Yeah," she said. "Daddy might've done that. It would be like him. Well, I think we need to have a talk with Tobe and see if he can tell us anything else. Do you know why Daddy went to the mine office?"

"He didn't say, miss. He just told me to saddle him up a horse. Said he was going to the mine office. That's all he said."

"I want to see Tobe as soon as possible," Marla said, "and I want you to ride with me over to the mine office tomorrow. First thing. I want to find out why Daddy went over there."

"Yes, ma'am."

Rance stood up to take his leave. He carried his hat in his hands until he reached the front door. Then he put the hat on and opened the door. He opened his mouth to say good night but stopped, mouth open.

"Miss Marla," he said.

"What?"

"Rider coming. He's leading a horse. Looks like something on the other horse." Marla stood and hurried over to the door. She and Rance went out onto the porch. "Looks like a body slung across the saddle," Rance went on. Then he recognized Slocum's Appaloosa. "Well, I'll be damned," he said. "Miss Marla, that's John Slocum." Rance's hand went to the butt of his revolver.

"Leave it, Rance," said Marla.

Slocum rode on up to the porch.

"Who's that?" Rance asked, nodding toward the limp form draped across the other horse.

"Sheriff," Slocum said, dismounting.

"Dead?"

"He was alive when I loaded him up," said Slocum. "I ain't slowed down to check since then."

Slocum was already by the sheriff's side untying the rope that held him on the saddle. Rance hurried to give him a hand. Together they slipped the body down.

"Bring him inside," Marla said.

Rance and Slocum carried the sheriff into the house and followed Marla to a bedroom where they laid him out on the bed. Slocum laid his head down on Johnson's chest.

"He's breathing," he said.

"Rance," said Marla, "send someone to town for the doc, fast."

"Yes, ma'am," said Rance. He turned and ran for the front door. Marla pushed Slocum aside so that she could examine the wound. She looked up at Slocum.

"You do this?" she asked.

"You mean the shooting or the patching?" he asked.

"Both."

"I didn't do the shooting," he said. "I did the patching. It ain't the best, but then, it wasn't the best of circumstances we was in."

"You did a pretty good job," she said. "I'm going to get some hot water and some fresh bandages. You stay here with him."

Marla left the room, and Slocum pulled a chair up beside the bed. He stared down at Burl Johnson, amazed that the man still had life in him. He was one tough son of a bitch. Then he wondered at the reception he had received from Rance and from this woman, who he figured must be ole Ziggie's daughter. He considered that they could be setting him up. Take care of Johnson first. Act like it's okay for Slocum to be there. Then when the doc shows up, and the emergency with Johnson is in the hands of the doc, have some cowhands slip in and cover Slocum with their Colts. He thought that he might be better off to get out while the getting was good. He had done his duty. He had brought Johnson in alive. Why hang around and take more chances?

Marla came back into the room, and Slocum got up and out of her way. She went to work unwrapping the work that Slocum had done. Then she dipped a rag into the hot water and started bathing the wound.

"It's a nasty one," she said.

"Rifle shot," said Slocum. "From some distance. Hit him in the back and come out the front."

"I can see that," she said. "If he lives, he's going to be down for a good long spell."

"I got him here as quick as I could," Slocum said. "It was shorter to here than it would've been to town from where we was at."

"You did right to bring him here," Marla said. She put aside the rag and the water bowl, ready to wrap fresh bandages around the wound. "Help me here," she said. Together they lifted Johnson enough to allow Marla to wind strips of bandage around his chest and back. At last, she was done, and they let him down again. Marla tied the ends of the bandage.

"There," she said. "Doc will probably redo it all when he gets here."

"It'll sure do till then," said Slocum. "You done a good job there."

"Thanks. By the way, I'm Marla. Ziggie's daughter."

"I figured that," said Slocum. He held out a hand, and Marla took it. "I'm John Slocum."

"I know. Rance told me when he saw you riding up."

"Did he tell you—"

"That they suspected you of killing Daddy? Yes. He told me. Did you?"

"No."

"I didn't think so."

"What makes you say that? You don't even know me."

"We talked over all the circumstances," she said. "It didn't make sense."

"Well, I appreciate that," Slocum said. "No one else seemed to want to talk over anything. They just wanted to keep yelling out that I done it."

"Do you have any ideas?"

"I know who done it," Slocum said. "I can't prove it in court though."

"Tell me."

Slocum looked Marla in the face. It was a young and lovely face. He could tell that, in spite of the fact that it wore a hard-set expression just then. He had seldom seen such a look on the face of a young woman. It was a look that said she wanted the man who had killed her father. She wanted revenge. Not justice. Revenge. He couldn't blame her for that.

"It was Tobe," Slocum said. "He killed Ziggie. Myron saw it done, and he told me. Then Tobe killed him. I explained it all to the sheriff, and then someone picked him off from ambush. I'm sure that was Tobe too. Like I said, I can't prove a word of it."

Marla heaved a heavy sigh and stood up. She looked down at Johnson. Then she looked at Slocum.

"There's nothing more we can do here," she said. "We're just waiting for Doc. How about a whiskey?"

"I wouldn't mind," Slocum said, and he followed Marla

into the big, main room. She gestured toward a large, stuffed chair, and Slocum sat down. Marla poured two glasses of whiskey, took one to Slocum, then sat in a chair facing him. She lifted her glass as if for a toast. Slocum lifted his in response, and they drank.

"Thanks," he said. "It's good whiskey, and I sure did need it."

"I imagine you've had a rough time of it," Marla said.

"It ain't been none too easy on you."

"It's not exactly the homecoming I imagined," she said. She sipped her drink. "So it was Tobe."

"I said I can't prove it."

"Will you try?"

Slocum gave Marla a curious look.

"I've heard that you're a hell of a gunfighter," she said. "And I've heard that you don't like hiring out your gun. Unless you know you're on the right side. Will you work for me? Will you try to prove that Tobe's guilty?"

"I might not be able to do that," Slocum said.

"Just do your best, and if you can't get enough proof for a court of law, just get enough to convince me. That's all I ask."

"Then what?"

She shrugged. "You don't like to hire out your gun. Okay. Just prove to me that Tobe's guilty, and you can ride off. I'll take care of the rest. If I can't prove him guilty in court and watch him hang, I'll kill him myself."

Slocum felt a chill run over his skin as he looked at Marla. He tossed down the rest of his whiskey. She would kill a man, he thought. She'd do it in a minute. Well, by God, she had good reason, and he agreed with her. If there was not enough evidence for a trial, the law would let Tobe go. A back-shooting bastard like Tobe had not ought to be let go.

"I'll work for you," he said. "And I won't ride out once I've convinced you that Tobe's the one. I won't ride out on you."

Marla stood up and got the whiskey bottle. She poured Slocum a refill and smiled at him. "Thanks," she said.

6

When Doc Smiley came out of the bedroom, followed by his part-time nurse, Hettie, Slocum and Marla both stood up anxiously. Doc put his bag on a small table, took off and folded up his glasses, and tucked them into a pocket. He looked up at the two waiting there for some word from him on the condition of Burl Johnson. Times like this, Doc felt terribly inadequate, but he was all people had to rely on, and he knew it.

"Well?" Marla said. "How is he?"

"Not good," said Doc. "He'd be a whole lot worse, though, if you two hadn't done what you did. Might be you saved his life. We won't know for sure for a while though. Right now, all we can do is wait."

"Is he still unconscious?" Slocum asked.

"Yeah. He could be like that for some time. I've done all I can do for now. I'll come back around tomorrow and check on him. In the meantime, Hettie here will stay around and watch over him. If that's all right with you, Marla. It wouldn't be safe to move him into town just now."

"Sure it's okay," Marla said. "They're both welcome here. Thanks, Doc." She walked to the door with him and said good night. Then she turned back to face Hettie. "Is there anything you need?" she asked.

"No, thank you. I've got all I need for now."

"Let me show you where things are in the kitchen. You might have to shift for yourself around here tomorrow."

Hettie followed Marla to the kitchen, and Slocum helped himself to another drink. Then he sat down again. He felt his pocket for a cigar, but he remembered that he had taken out his last two just before the sheriff had been shot. He must have dropped them out there. He wished that he had another. Marla and Hettie came back out of the kitchen, and Hettie went back into the room with her patient. Marla sat down with a heavy sigh.

"You know," Slocum said, "if he don't wake up, you got nothing but my word that I didn't shoot him. Ziggie too for that matter."

"I'll take your word," she said. "If you shot him, why would you bring him back here?"

Slocum shrugged. "Make myself look good?"

"No. You're no doctor. You wouldn't know if he was likely to come around or not. If he did come around, and if it was you who did the shooting, then he'd tell. No. You didn't do it. And we know you didn't kill Myron. There are witnesses to that one."

"What about Ziggie?"

She looked at him. Then she shook her head. "No," she said. "It was Tobe. All the way. We both know that."

"With the sheriff laid up the way he is," Slocum said, "is there any law around here?"

"Burl didn't have a deputy. The town thought it was saving money, and there hadn't been any serious trouble around here for quite a spell. Nothing that Burl couldn't handle anyway."

"So how do we handle this situation? Take the law into our own hands?"

"For right now," Marla said, "let's just nose around some. We'll figure out just what to do about it later. It's late, and I'm tired. You must be too. There's a spare room down the hall there. It's yours."

"Is that a good idea?" Slocum asked.

"It's the best one I can think of," she answered. "Do all the hands believe that you're not Daddy's killer? Has anyone even talked to them about it? I've talked to Rance, and I think that he agrees with me now, but I don't know if he's talked to anyone else yet. You might not be safe in the bunkhouse, and you can't go to town. All anyone there knows for sure is that you cracked Burl's skull and broke out of jail."

"I guess you're right," Slocum said. "I'll just go out and take care of my horse and get my bedroll."

"I'll walk out with you," she said. "Just in case you run into someone out there."

Marla stepped out onto the porch early the next morning ready to ride just as Rance, leading two saddled horses, was approaching the house from the corral. "Good morning," she said.

"Morning, ma'am," said Rance. "Ready to go?"

"Who's the extra horse for?"

"I figgered I'd ride along with you. After what happened—"

"I'll be taking Slocum along," she said.

Rance thought a moment before answering. "I think he'll have to saddle his own horse," he said, "unless he wants to ride this one."

"Have you told Tobe that I want to see him?"

"I ain't seen him since I sent him back from the posse. He might be hanging out at the mine office."

"What business does he have over there? He's a cowhand, isn't he?"

"Yes, ma'am, but he gets along pretty well with ole Charlie Dode, and I reckon he's kinda pouting at me over the last words we had. He might be over there."

Just then Slocum stepped out on the porch.

"You ready to ride?" Marla asked.

"Soon as I saddle my horse," Slocum said.

"Give him a rest," said Marla. "He had a hard day yesterday too. Ride this one."

Slocum looked at the horse and at Rance. "Okay," he said.

Marla and Slocum mounted up, and Rance said, "I'll look around for Tobe, but you might run into him over at the mine. Be careful."

"I'll be watching," Slocum said.

Rance stood for a moment watching them ride down the lane. Then he turned to walk back to the corral and saddle himself another horse. He had Tobe to look for, and he had ranch business to take care of. There was a killer loose, but the ranch still had to be run. If Miss Marla wanted to ride around the countryside with John Slocum, what business of his was it anyhow?

Slocum and Marla rode along for a while in silence. It was obvious to Slocum that Marla was in charge. She had made that obvious. He decided that he would keep his mouth shut and let her do the talking at the mine office. He had not even met Dode, and if they should run into Tobe out there, Slocum figured that keeping his trap shut was the only way to keep from getting into a fight. Marla wasn't ready for that yet. So he would keep quiet. He was going along to make sure that she was safe. That was all. But if anyone started anything, he could damn well finish it.

It came into his mind that it would be a simple and easy thing to provoke Tobe into a fight and just kill the son of a bitch and get it all over with. It came into his mind, but he put it right out again. There were a couple of things wrong with that reasoning. First of all, it would leave a little doubt in some minds as to whether Tobe or Slocum had actually killed Ziggie. He didn't want to ride away from the place with any doubt in anyone's mind.

The second problem was that neither Slocum nor anyone else had figured out any reason for Tobe to have done the killing. No one, that is, except Myron. So much had happened that Slocum had almost forgotten what Myron had said.

"Marla."

"Yes?"

"It just come back to me what ole Myron told me out there that night."

"He said that he saw Tobe shoot Daddy, didn't he?"

"Yeah, and more. He said that he heard Ziggie say something like, 'He's robbing me blind.' "

"Yeah, I remember you said that. Was he talking about Charlie Dode?"

"That was all Myron heard. Right after that, Tobe pulled out his gun and shot Ziggie. But Myron figured that Ziggie must've been talking about Dode. He had just come from the mine office."

"If Myron was right," said Marla, "then Tobe must be in on it, whatever it is, with Dode. Rance told me that those two are pretty tight. Slocum, don't say anything about this. Not yet. I'm not going to let on to Dode or Tobe that I'm suspicious of them. I'll just ask a few questions and see what kind of reaction I get. That's all."

"Don't worry about me," said Slocum. "I'll just hang back. It's your game, and I'll let you play it."

Charlie Dode looked out the window of his office and saw the two riders coming along the road below. He stood up and stepped over to the window for a better look. "Tobe," he said, "who's this coming?" Tobe was lounging with a drink on the other side of the room. He got up with a moan and trudged over to stand beside Dode and look out. He waited a moment as the riders came closer. Then his hand went to his six-gun.

"That's Slocum," he said.

Dode put a hand on Tobe's wrist. "Don't get anxious," he said. "There's a gal with him. Who could she be?"

Tobe squinted. "I don't know her," he said, "but I heared that ole Ziggie's daughter was a-coming in. She'd be the boss now, I reckon. Maybe that's her."

"Well, now, let's step out and greet them," Dode said.

"But Slocum—"

"Stay calm," said Dode. "Let me handle things. I'll let you know when it's time for—that."

Dode led the way out the door, and he and Tobe stood on the small porch looking down onto the road there where it came to an end at the foot of the stairs that led up to the mine office. Down below, Marla and Slocum stopped their horses and looked up.

"Howdy," Dode called. "You Slocum?"

"I am."

"And you'd be   "

"I'm Marla Ziglinsky."

"I'm Charlie Dode, and this here is Tobe. Come on up."

Slocum and Marla dismounted and climbed the stairs. Then they followed Dode and Tobe into the office. Slocum took a quick look around. Everything seemed normal for a mine office. A safe sat against one wall. The desk was cluttered with papers. A table across the room held a few papers. An old Sharps buffalo gun stood in one corner of the room. Slocum could see from across the room that it hadn't been used in a while. It was covered with dust. Dode gestured toward two chairs. Marla and Slocum sat down. Dode offered drinks, but only Tobe accepted the offer. Then he offered cigars, and Slocum took one. He'd been craving one anyhow. Might as well smoke one of Dode's. As Slocum puffed on his cigar to get it going, Dode said, "What can I do for you?"

"I just got home," Marla said. "Since I found out that I'm in charge here now—"

"Oh, yes," said Dode. "A terrible thing about your father. Please accept my condolences."

"Yes," she said. "Thanks. As I was saying, since I found out I'm in charge now, I thought I'd look the place over. I've never been over to the mine. Daddy really just got it going while I was away. I wanted to meet you, Mr. Dode—"

"Charlie, please."

"I wanted to meet you and ask how things are going."

"Well, Miss Marla," said Dode, "I wish I could give you a better story, but you know, like you said, this is a fairly new operation here, and it takes a while to get things going the way you want them to go. I know that Ziggie, uh, your father, was not pleased, but I explained to him just what I told you. Give me another four to six weeks, and you'll see it start to pick up right smart."

"Daddy wasn't happy with the mine operations?"

"Well, you know what I mean. He was anxious for the mine to start showing a huge profit, and I'm afraid that it's still operating in the red. A new business and all. I tried to explain it to him so he'd understand."

"But he didn't?"

"I hope that he did, but Ziggie was a cow man. He had no experience with mines. He just didn't understand what all's involved here."

"But you have experience with mines?"

"Oh yes. I've run several successful operations."

"And how do you feel about this one?"

"Like I said, give me another six weeks, maybe less, and we'll start to show a substantial profit. I'm well pleased with our progress here."

"Well, then," said Marla, "since you're the expert, I'd say that yours is the opinion that counts. That's really all I wanted to hear. Except about the day that Daddy was killed. He had come out here to visit with you, I believe."

"Yes, he had. Tobe here rode out with him."

"I heard that much," said Marla. "Why did he come out here?"

"Like I told you, he was disappointed in the progress of the mine. I explained it to him the best I could. Just as I did to you."

"And then he left—alone?"

"Yes," said Dode. "He had told Tobe to ride on back earlier."

"Said he didn't need no nursemaid," Tobe added.

"So he was alone when he was ambushed, and there were no witnesses," Marla said.

"That's right," said Dode. "As far as I know. He left here alone."

"Thank you very much," Marla said. "We'll be running along now and let you get back to work here. I don't want to slow things down any more than they are already."

"You're riding along in the company of the mainest suspect in the killing of your daddy," said Tobe, pointing a finger at Slocum. "Them two had a fight just before that. Slocum was arrested, and he broke jail. We went after him in a posse."

"I've heard all about that," Marla said. "But Slocum's been released by the sheriff. He's no longer a suspect."

"But how—"

"Never mind, Tobe," said Dode. "Slocum, it's been a pleasure. I'm sure we'll meet again. Miss Marla, I hope that I'll have better news for you the next time I see you."

"Thank you," said Marla, and she and Slocum walked out the door. Dode walked over to the window and watched as they descended the long stairway.

"Why'd you shoosh me up?" Tobe asked.

"Marla has obviously sided with Slocum for her own reasons. She already knows that he was a suspect in the killing, but she says that he's not any longer. There's no point in us getting into an open argument about it with them. Let it go, but keep your eyes and ears open."

"You think they suspect anything?"

"I don't think so, but like I said, don't let's get caught off guard."

"Say, Charlie, whenever did ole Burl Johnson say that about Slocum? I thought I killed Burl."

"I thought you had too," Dode said. "Do you suppose Slocum brought him back alive?"

"Slocum," asked Marla, "what do you think?"

"They're a pair of lying dogs," Slocum said. "I know that Tobe killed Ziggie, and I know he killed Myron. I'm convinced that he shot Johnson too."

"And Charlie Dode and the mine?"

"I believe that he's hauling plenty of silver out of there," said Slocum, "but I doubt if it's showing on the books."

"How can we prove that?"

"You study up on the books," he said, "and how about I

sneak out here after dark and spy around and see what I can see?"

"If you think that's the way to do it, then let's do it. When do we start?"

"Tonight."

"All right. I'll feed you a good supper first back at the ranch house."

"That sounds fine with me."

"Do you think that Charlie Dode has an inkling that we're suspicious of him?"

"He's hard to read," Slocum said, "but I don't think so. I think he thinks that we're just dumb, and he can get away with most anything he wants to."

"Let's try to keep it that way for a spell."

"I agree. That's the best way."

"Slocum," she said.

"Yes, ma'am?"

"One thing Charlie Dode didn't know."

"What's that?"

"Daddy had plenty of mining experience. Years ago when he was younger. That's how he got the money to buy this spread. From mining."

They were met on the porch by Hettie, and after greetings, Marla asked, "Any change?"

Hettie shook her head. "No change," she said. "Doc came out for a while. He changed the bandage. Nothing more we can do, he said. Just wait it out."

Marla sighed. "Well," she said, "I'll get supper started."

"Wait up," said Slocum. "Looky there."

Marla turned and saw that Slocum was pointing toward Rance, who was headed for the ranch house at a run.

"Rance," Marla said. "What is it?"

Rance stopped just at the bottom of the steps. He stood panting. "Couple of the boys just rode in," he said. "From the north range. They said, near as they can tell, there's seventy-five to a hundred head missing from up there."

"Missing?"

"Looks like rustlers."

"Oh, damn," said Marla. "That's all we need now."

Slocum thought hard. Ziggie had just been murdered. Probably Charlie Dode was stealing silver from the mine. Ziggie suspected it, and that's why he was killed. Tobe did it on Dode's instructions. The ranch had a new boss, and it was Marla. She was Ziggie's daughter, but Slocum did not figure that she had much experience at running a ranch and a mine. Now rustlers. He wondered, was all that connected somehow? If so, was Dode behind the rustling as well as the theft at the mine? Was Tobe involved in rustling?

It would be interesting to know just when the cattle had disappeared. And where they had been taken. He decided that he would ride out on the trail of the stolen cattle and see what he could see. If he could get back in time to hide out and watch the mine, he'd do that too. If not, well, he'd do that another night.

"Well," said Marla to Rance, "what do you propose we do?"

"I'd like to take some of the boys out for a look around," Rance said.

"I'd like to go along," said Slocum.

Rance looked at Marla. She nodded.

"All right," she said. "To both of you."

"Say," Slocum said, "do we know how long the cattle have been missing?"

"Well, no," said Rance. "We don't rightly know that."

"Then why not just the three of us ride out in the morning? No sense in taking a whole damn crew just to look things over. Maybe they been gone a week or more. We'd just waste a lot of hours."

"That makes sense to me, Rance," said Marla. "Put someone in charge in the morning, and the three of us will ride out and look around."

7

They rode the range for several hours in the general area where the missing cattle should have been. Slocum was beginning to wonder if Rance was full of shit. He wondered if the cattle simply wandered onto another part of the ranch and blended in with others. He was about to suggest a total inventory of cattle on the ranch, when he heard Rance shout. He looked up to see the foreman waving his hat in the air. The three riders had separated in order to cover more ground, so Slocum headed for Rance across the way, and he noticed that Marla was doing the same. Marla reached Rance a little before Slocum, and as soon as Slocum rode up, Rance pointed at the ground.

"They rounded them up right here," he said.

"Sure looks that way," Slocum agreed. "Let's see how far we can follow the trail."

They rode along together for a while in silence. At last Rance spoke up.

"Pretty bold rustlers," he said. "They sure didn't do much to hide their trail."

"It's fresh too," said Marla.

"Could be they thought with Ziggie out of the way, no one would follow them," Slocum said. "Or it could be that they mean to get across the territorial line to sell them. They'd figure the law couldn't follow them over there."

"Maybe the law can't," Marla said, "but we can. Should we go back and get some more hands?"

Rance looked over at Slocum. "How many rustlers do you make it?" he asked.

"At least four," Slocum said. "Could be more."

"We ought to get some help then," Rance said. "Even if we could take them, there's a right smart number of cows for just the two of us to handle."

"Three," Marla said.

"Yes, ma'am," Rance said. "It's still a right smart number."

"All right," she said. "Let's hurry on back to the ranch and round up some of the boys."

"Why don't you two hurry on back?" Slocum suggested. "I'll keep on the trail in case it should play out somewhere along the way. If it does, I'll make sure to mark my trail for you to follow."

"If you come on them before we get back to you," Marla said, "don't try anything by yourself."

"I'm no fool," Slocum said.

"We'll be back as fast as we can," Marla said. Then to Rance, she said, "Let's go."

Slocum didn't bother looking over his shoulder to watch them ride away. He continued on the trail. There was something funny going on. Almost as if someone out there was trying to break the Circle Z. Old Ziggie had been murdered, likely because he had discovered some serious diverting of ore from his mine. It could be, he thought, that someone, almost surely that damn Charlie Dode, was simply trying to line his own pockets with the old man's money. But now some cattle had been stolen. Well, there were rustlers around. Always and anywhere you might go. Still, an awful lot of bad things were happening to the Circle Z all at once.

He rode till nightfall, rode on some more, then stopped for a few hours sleep. He was up at the crack of dawn riding again. He hoped that the rustlers spent more time sleeping than he did. He knew that he was making better time than they were. A herd of cattle can only be moved along so fast, but he also knew that they had a head start on him. The trail was still abundantly clear, but there was no sign of them ahead. He rode on.

As he rode, he thought of Marla Ziglinsky. She was a determined woman who showed a good share of her father's determination and tough spirit. Lots of women in her position would be sitting at home weeping and bemoaning their sad fortune. Not her. Marla was on the trail of killers and ore thieves and cattle rustlers. She was determined that no one was going to get away with any of that, not at her expense. And where most everyone in the area, including Rance and the sheriff, had been ready to watch Slocum hang for Ziggie's killing, she had given the matter some thought. She had never believed that he was the guilty one. He had to like her for that.

And it wasn't difficult liking Marla Ziglinsky. She was a fine-looking woman, in addition to all her other admirable qualities. He wasn't sure of her age, but she couldn't be thirty, he thought. She had smooth auburn hair, big brown eyes, and full, pouting lips. Her breasts were ample, her waist narrow, and her hips—well, she was just a fine-looking woman from head to toe. And she could sit a horse and ride with the best of them.

Slocum did not feel guilty or negligent about his musings as he rode along, for the trail was wide and obvious, and he could see well ahead. He wondered how soon he would be able to actually see the herd or the rustlers or even the dust rising behind them. He wasn't worried though. He didn't really want to see them too soon. He needed Marla and Rance to return with help before he could take them on. If he should come up on the herd and the rustlers still alone, he would simply have to hold back, keeping himself out of sight while keeping them in sight and waiting for the cowhands to arrive.

He passed the rest of the day in that manner, riding along following the trail, musing about the attacks on the Circle Z, and thinking about the enchanting Marla Z. Just as he had done the night before, he rode for a while into the night before stopping for a few hours to grab some shut-eye. In the morning, he got up and stretched and prepared to ride some more. As he threw the saddle on his horse's back, he wished that he had some eggs and bacon and biscuits. Barring all that, he sure did wish he had some coffee. He mounted up and rode after the herd.

Around noon that day, Slocum saw the dust trail. He increased his pace a little. It wasn't long before he could hear the lowing complaints of the cattle and now and then the whoops of the rustlers. He followed carefully. Finally, he decided that he was getting in too big a hurry. There was no need for him to catch up so fast. He had them in his sights, and he had help coming up from behind. He decided to drop back a ways in order to keep from eating their dust. He followed the herd in that manner until late into the evening.

It was not yet dark, but the light in the sky was low and dim when the rustlers stopped the herd for the night and made their camp. Slocum waited for the dust ahead to settle. Then he moved in a little closer, taking care not to expose himself. He found a grove of trees just ahead of a small hill, and he hid the big Appaloosa in the trees and walked on ahead. Scrambling up to the top of the rise, he surveyed the rustlers' camp. He could see them pretty well, and he did not recognize any of them. Perhaps, he thought, they would not recognize him either.

He snaked down the backside of the hill and made his way back to his horse. Then he mounted up and rode straight for the rustlers' camp. Some of the men stiffened when they saw him coming, and a few hands went to the butts of their six-guns. Even the men sitting on the ground with plates of beans stopped shoveling food into their mouths and sat with their eyes trained on him. Slocum rode up close before he stopped.

"Howdy," he said. "Can you fellas spare a cup of coffee for a weary traveler?"

He knew that he had put them on the spot. If they drove him away, they would give themselves away. No honest cow camp would turn away a stranger. He watched as two of the men exchanged furtive looks, and one of them gave the other a nod. Then they looked back at Slocum.

"Climb on down, stranger," said the one who had received the nod. "Come on in and set."

As he swung down out of the saddle, Slocum was conscious of a dozen eyeballs trained suspiciously and warily on him and of six-gun hands itching to slap leather. He was in a rustlers' camp. There was no doubt about that. He let the reins trail in the dust, and the big stallion waited patiently. Slocum ambled over close to the fire. One of the rustlers handed him a tin cup. It was hot to the touch, but the coffee in it sure smelled good.

"Thanks," said Slocum.

"Pot of beans on the fire over yonder," the man said. "Plate's right beside it. Help yourself."

"I reckon I will," Slocum said. "Mighty kind of you. Thanks."

He got himself a plate, dipped out some beans and sat down. Some of the rustlers had gone back to feeding their own faces, but the two who had invited him into the camp kept watching him carefully. He finished his beans, then moved back to the coffeepot with his cup. Motioning toward the pot, he looked at the two sullen hands.

"Mind?" he said.

"Go ahead," one of the men said.

Slocum poured himself another cup of coffee. He sat down and blew on the hot liquid. Then he took a loud sip. He looked up again.

"You boys got to drive your herd far?" he asked.

"Not far," said one. "Another day or so is all."

"You don't need a new hand, do you?"

"Nope. We got a full crew."

Slocum shrugged. "No harm in asking," he said. "Know of anywhere a cowhand might find a job? I can herd cattle, bust broncs, or mend fence. Hell, it don't matter to me."

"I don't know of anyplace," said one of the men, just as another stepped in out of the shadows to look sideways at Slocum.

"What's your name?" the newcomer asked.

Slocum looked the man in the face for a moment. "Usually that ain't a polite question in these parts," he said, "but I don't mind. I'm Slocum."

"I thought so," the man from the shadows said. "Don't you work for the Circle Z?"

"I did."

"What happened?"

"Ole Ziggie fired me," Slocum said. "I got crossways with another hand over my horse. Then Ziggie got hisself killed, and the law come after me for it."

"You do it?"

"If I did," said Slocum, "you reckon I'd own up to it that easy?"

The other sniggered, and said, "I reckon not." Then he sidled up to one of his companions and talked into the side of the man's head in a low tone. Slocum acted as if he wasn't interested, and in fact, he was asking himself why the hell he had intruded into this camp of rustlers in the first place. Maybe he had just wanted a closer look at them. Or a look at the cows to check the brand and thereby double-check his own conviction that these bastards had actually stolen Circle Z cattle. But finally he admitted to himself that he had just been craving some coffee and food. Now he had a problem: how to extricate himself safely from this den of thieves.

He wondered how much longer it would take Rance, and likely Marla, to get there with help, and then he thought that if he didn't get himself out of this, he could easily be caught in the middle of a shoot-out. That was not a pleasant prospect. He stood up and stretched.

"That feels a whole lot better, boys," he said. "I sure do thank you for your hospitality. Now I guess I'll be riding on."

"Where you headed?" one of the rustlers asked.

"Like I said, looking for work."

"You ain't going to find it in the middle of the night."

"You're right about that," Slocum said, "but I might get myself closer to a ranch somewhere with some promise."

"Stick around," said the other. "You might just as well spend the night here and head out early in the morning."

Slocum hesitated. These men were still suspicious of him. If he tried to ride out, he might just get a bullet in the back. "Well," he said, "I'm obliged to you again. I just didn't want to impose myself on you any longer is all. I'll just unsaddle my horse and get my bedroll."

He walked over to the Appaloosa to do what he had said. Pretty soon, he had his bedroll laid out on the ground. He sat down on it, pulled off his boots, then stretched himself out.

"This is a whole lot better than riding off into the night," he said.

"Yeah," said the rustler. "You ain't got to worry about nothing. You got plenty of men around you. Hell, you can just sleep like a baby."

Slocum did not sleep right away, and when he did, he went to sleep wondering about Rance and Marla and trying to figure out just what he would do if shooting started while he was still in the midst of the rustlers. He couldn't be sure just how long he had been asleep, but it had been awhile. Slocum was a light sleeper, and he woke up when he heard someone rummaging through his saddlebags. He slipped the Colt out of its holster and thumbed back the hammer, and the culprit straightened up.

"I thought you all were mighty hospitable," Slocum said, "but searching through my stuff like that ain't friendly."

"Hold on now," said the sneak, extending his arms out to his sides. "Don't get trigger-happy."

"Just what the hell were you looking for anyhow?"

"Just checking," the man said. "You can't be too careful, you know. How the hell do we know you're who you say you are?"

"Nothing in them bags will prove it to you one way or the other," said Slocum, "and if you meant to rob me, you wouldn't find anything worth stealing in there either."

He sat up, still holding the six-gun on the man, and with his left hand, he pulled on his boots. Then he stood up and gathered his belongings under his left arm. It was awkward, but he walked with them over to the Appaloosa. The man looked over his shoulder.

"Where you going?"

"Try to find a place where folks are more friendly," said Slocum. He was trying to figure out how he could get the saddle on the Appaloosa with saddlebags and blanket under one arm and a gun in the other hand. "Come on over here," he said, "and move quiet. Don't wake up your buddies."

The man walked carefully over to where Slocum waited beside his horse.

"Now," said Slocum, "loosen your gun belt and let it down to the ground real easy." The man did as he'd been told. "Now you can throw the blanket and saddle on my horse for me."

He held his Colt ready and watched while the rustler saddled up the Appaloosa, tied on the saddlebags, and rolled and strapped on the blanket roll. Slocum checked the cinch to make sure it was tight enough.

"Now walk back over there by the fire," he said, "away from your six-gun."

The man walked away, and Slocum swung himself up into the saddle. He turned his horse and rode away quickly. Almost immediately he heard voices behind him as the other rustlers came awake in confusion. No one bothered coming after him though. He was glad to be away from them. He wondered what the others were saying to the clumsy oaf who had awakened him and then let him get away.

He rode back the way he had come, thinking that he might come across the Circle Z crew that way. The trail was well pounded down by the herd of stolen cattle, and he was able to move along pretty well even in the dark. He had gone no more than a couple of miles when he saw a faint glimmer ahead. A campfire maybe. Maybe Rance and the others. But maybe not. He rode on cautiously. Ready for anything. He looked behind him and listened carefully. There was still no sign of pursuit. Maybe the rustlers figured it was just as well to be rid of him.

Drawing closer to the light ahead, he could see that it was indeed a campfire. He moved ahead slow and easy. Then a voice came out of the darkness.

"You out there," it said. "Stop where you are."

Slocum stopped and waited. Then he heard another voice talking to the first one, and he thought that he recognized it. "Is that you, Rance?" he called out.

"Slocum?"

"It's me."

"Ride on in."

Slocum moved forward. Rance, unlike the sloppy rustlers, had posted a guard for the night. That was good. For the second time the same night, Slocum unsaddled his horse and laid out his bedroll, but he did not go right to sleep. The entire Circle Z crew was up and awake and anxious to hear what he had to say.

"They're right up ahead," he told them, "and they ain't being too cautious. They camped behind the cows, so I never really got a look at brands."

"We already know they're ours," said Rance. "We've been right on their trail all the way from the ranch."

"I went in a few hours ago and ate their beans and drank their coffee. There's six of them, best I can tell. I don't believe they had anyone out night riding. Like I said, they're right careless." He looked around the camp. Rance and Marla were there, along with Tobe and eight other cowhands. "They're hardcases," he said, "but I think we can take them easy enough."

"If they're like you say," Marla said, "lazy-like, they probably won't be up and at it too early."

"I get your meaning," Rance said. "If we got ourselves up before daylight, we could hit them by surprise. Do you think they'll fight?"

"It's hard to say," said Slocum. "If we for sure get the drop on them, they might just cave in."

"I say shoot first and ask questions later," Tobe piped in. "Why take chances?"

"Yeah," said Slocum. "That's your style, ain't it?"

"Better safe than sorry."

"Tobe," said Rance, "you hold your fire till you see me shoot. You hear? If you fire the first shot, I'll kill you myself. You got that?"

"I hear you," Tobe said, and he muttered to himself, but loudly enough to be heard, "Shit."

"Well," Marla said, "if we're going to get after them early, I suggest we all get some sleep. We need to be at our best. There's no telling what might happen in the morning."

Slocum looked at Marla and saw that she was wearing a six-gun. He smiled. Every time he learned something more about her, he liked her all the better. He sat on his bedroll and pulled off his boots again. Then he stretched out. Yes, indeed, he thought, that Marla was some fine woman.

8

Slocum felt secure there in the camp of the Circle Z with a sentry on watch posted by Rance, and he soon dozed off. He was thinking about the lovely Marla Ziglinsky as he fell into a deep slumber. Soon he found himself snoozing in a big feather bed. He felt a touch on his shoulder, and he rolled over and opened his eyes to see Marla standing there in the room, smiling down at him, and he realized that she was stark, staring naked. He looked at her in all her loveliness, and he tossed the covers aside. He too was naked, and he was more than ready for her with his stiff rod standing straight up to attention.

"I been wondering how long it would take you to come to me," he said.

"I wanted to," she said, "from the first time I saw you. I've just been waiting for the right moment."

"I guess you found it," Slocum said. He reached out a hand, and she took it, and he pulled her toward him. She put one knee on the big, fluffy mattress, reached for his shoulders with both hands, and swung her other leg up and over him as if she were mounting a saddled horse. In position, she reached down with one hand to guide his hungry cock into her waiting, wet tunnel of love. As she placed the head of his throbbing tool in between her luscious, silky vaginal lips, Slocum moaned out loud with the intense pleasure.

He reached up, taking her breasts in his hands, and he fondled the nipples with his thumbs, causing them to stand out hard, as she lowered herself along the full length of his anxious tool. At last, she settled down, sitting her bare ass on the tops of his thighs, his long, hard cock jammed far up inside her. She scooted forward and groaned. Then she moved back. She thrust herself forward and back again, and then she began rocking away faster and faster and moaning louder with each thrust. Slocum squeezed her lovely tits, content for the time being to allow her to do the work. It was obvious that she too was content with things the way they were.

"Oh, God," she said suddenly. "God, Slocum, I'm coming. I'm coming. I'm coming."

She rocked more violently, faster and harder for a few more strokes, and then she stopped, threw back her head and took several deep breaths. At last, she fell forward, pressing her breasts against his bare chest and her lips against his. It was their first kiss, and it was long and hard, and then her lips parted, and his did too, and they began to duel with their tongues. Slocum waited as long as he could stand it before rolling her over. Now he was on top, and they were still joined together. He began to thrust, slowly at first, then harder and faster.

"Ah," she cried, as she built up to a second frenzy, but Slocum stopped with no warning and pulled out. She looked at him, puzzled, and started to say something, but he reached down, grabbing her waist, and he turned her over onto her stomach, then pulled her up onto her knees. With one hand, he felt for her slimy hole, and with the other, he guided his greedy cock back into place. Then he held her hips tightly, and he pounded into her again and again. Her moans grew louder and louder.

Slocum felt the pressure building in his balls. He felt his cock engorged. Then suddenly came the release. He spurted into her depths again and again, and with each spurt, he banged against her round and beautiful ass. At last he was done, spent, worn completely out. He stayed himself behind her on his knees, waiting for his flaccid cock to slip out on its own, and when it did at last, he leaned sideways and fell down on the fluffy mattress by her side, gasping for breath. Feeling the need for nearness, he rolled toward her onto his side and reached out with his right arm, but when it fell, it did not encircle the naked loveliness of Marla Ziglinsky. Instead, it fell off the side of his bedroll onto the hard and cold ground.

"Ouch," he said out loud.

Slocum blinked his eyes, puzzled. He tried to bring back the image of what he had just done, but it was fast fading. He opened his eyes and looked around, discovering himself to be on the ground in the Circle Z camp, and Marla was nowhere near. It had all been a cruel dream, a fantasy, acted out in his sleep, and it was gone forever.

"Damn," he said, as he sat up and reached for his boots. He pulled them on and stood up to stretch. Then he finished dressing himself. He looked toward the campfire where the cook was busy preparing breakfast. Slocum could smell the boiling coffee, and he could see that several of the crew were already sipping from cups. He rolled up his blankets and went to the fire for his own.

Standing there by the fire with his cup, he looked around casually for Marla, but he did not see her. It was still dark, and there was time to spare. He wondered what she had dreamed during the night. Trying to appear nonchalant, he strolled to one side of the chuck wagon and looked around, and then he spotted her. She was seated on the ground on her bedroll there where she had rolled it out the night before behind he wagon. She was smiling and talking, and she was talking to—Rance.

Goddamn, Slocum said to himself. Rance. What the hell is going on here? When did that commence? Rance? He walked back to the fire where the cook was just scooping some bacon out of the pan.

"Breakfast, Slocum?"

"No. Hell no. I'd rather kill rustlers on a empty stomach.

I'm meaner when I'm hungry." He smelled the bacon though, and it sure did smell good. "Yeah," he said. "I changed my mind. I might need a little compassion out there this morning after all."

Soon everyone had eaten. They saddled their horses and mounted up, leaving behind the cook and his young assistant. They checked their weapons, and Slocum looked over at Marla. He had to remind himself that the dream was his alone. He was almost embarrassed to look at her. The sun was just beginning to show itself over the far eastern horizon.

"Well, Boss?" Slocum said.

"Let's go get them," Marla said.

They started riding toward the rustlers' camp, slowly at first, then as they drew nearer, they sped up. When the camp was in sight, they rode hard toward it, guns in hand.

"Hey," someone in the camp shouted. Rustlers were running in all directions. Three managed to get to saddled horses. They mounted up quickly and ran for their lives. The remaining three pulled out their weapons and fired at their attackers. Rance and some of the other Circle Z boys fired back, but their aims were bad from the backs of the racing horses. Slocum waited.

Near the camp, he hauled back on the reins and stopped the big Appaloosa. Then he whipped out his Colt and fired. His shot was off a bit, and he just nicked the shoulder of one of the rustlers, but it was enough to make the man scream and drop his gun. He turned to run, and he tripped. Turning again on all fours, he scrambled back for his gun. Picking it up, he thumbed back the hammer and aimed at Slocum. Slocum fired again. This time his bullet smashed into the man's forehead, dropping him like a sack. Slocum looked for another target, but he saw the other two men fall from Circle Z slugs. Marla led the way into the camp, now abandoned. The riders all dismounted. Rance turned the bodies over with the toe of his boot.

"Anyone know these bastards?" he asked.

No one did. He went through their pockets but found nothing of any interest. Then he started to rummage in the pockets of the three sets of saddlebags that were left lying there. He tossed aside the first two and was going through the last one. Some of the cowhands were pocketing the cash discovered on the bodies of the three men. One cowhand checked the boots of the three dead men, but discovered that his own boots were in much better shape than were theirs. He left the boots on the feet of the dead rustlers.

One cowhand stepped up to the fire and found the coffee still on. He located a clean-looking cup, and poured himself some. Slocum climbed back into the saddle. He rode around the camp looking for the tracks of the three who had fled. He discovered that they had taken off in different directions, and he decided that it would be a waste of time to try to follow any one of them.

"Hey," said Rance. "Look at this."

Slocum rode over beside him and looked down at what Rance was holding in his hand.

"It looks like a lump of silver ore to me," Slocum said.

"Would you say that this ties the rustlers in with Charlie Dode?" Marla asked.

"Well," said Rance, "it sure does tend to make me suspicious of ole Charlie."

"I'm convinced," Slocum said.

"It's circumstantial," Marla said. She held out her hand, and Rance dropped the lump of ore into her palm. She hefted it, then slipped it into a pocket. "I'll just hang onto it," she said. "A couple of you boys bury these three in shallow graves. Let's the rest of us get those cows headed back home."

As they moved the herd back toward home, Slocum kept watching Marla and Rance, looking for any sign of any kind of involvement other than that of ranch owner and foreman. He hadn't really read anything that way since his first look at them that morning, and that might not have meant anything. No telling what they were talking about, he said to himself. As for her smile, hell, maybe he said something funny. Then he thought that if ole Rance had done that, it would be the first time in history that he had showed any sense of humor at all.

Riding along beside the herd, Slocum remembered why he had stopped herding cattle. It was a dirty, dusty job. The cattle moved along too slowly, and you had to keep running the ornery, wild ones back in with the rest of the herd. It was not his idea of fun nor of a good time, and the wages were lousy anyhow. He looked back and noticed that Tobe was riding drag. He wondered if that had been Tobe's idea or if Rance had put him back there. Breathing in all that dust was good enough for the bastard, Slocum thought, but he did not really like the idea of having Tobe behind him.

Up ahead, he could see the chuck wagon still standing where they had left it that morning. He wondered if Marla and Rance would want to stop for a cup of coffee or just keep on keeping on toward home. He hoped they'd just keep on. He was already tired of this trail. Then he noticed that the fire had burned low. That seemed a little peculiar. He'd have thought that the cook would either have put the fire out or kept it going. One or the other. This was in between, and it did not make sense.

He heard Rance call out, "Keep 'em moving, boys," and saw him head off at an angle toward the campsite. Slocum turned to follow, as the herd was kept moving back toward the ranch. When Slocum caught up with Rance, they rode together toward the chuck wagon. Marla noticed them and rode to join them, just as they moved in close to the wagon.

"Oh, my God," Marla said, as she came in close enough to see.

The cook and his assistant were both lying dead beside the neglected fire. Both had been shot several times. Slocum began checking tracks. If there were any to be found, they would have to be found soon. He saw where two different horses had come into the camp from two different directions. Just before riding on in, they had joined up with one another.

"Damn," Rance said. He was off his horse, kneeling beside

the bodies. "This here was just puredee meanness. No reason for it at all."

"But who'd have done such a thing?" said Marla. "And why?"

"I'd say it was two of them rustlers that run off when we attacked," said Slocum. "They met up right here. Shot those two boys on accounta they were with us. That's all."

"Marla," said Rance, standing up, "I say we've put up with enough of this. I say we wipe them out, once and for all."

"I'm inclined to agree with you, Rance," she said. "We still don't have the kind of evidence you need to take to the law, but I'm convinced that Charlie Dode's behind it all."

"What do you say, Slocum?" Rance asked.

"I just do what I'm told to do," Slocum said. "I'm just a hired hand."

"You've got an opinion though."

"Charlie Dode's behind it all right," said Slocum. "I'm ready to go gunning for him any time Miss Marla says."

Not too far away, the herd finally passed, and as it did, Tobe turned his horse and rode over to join the other three at the wagon.

"What's happened here?" he said.

"What's it look like to you, Tobe?" said Slocum.

"Someone killed the boys."

"That's what it looks like to me too," Slocum said. "Who you reckon done a thing like that?"

"Why, how should I know? Couple a them rustlers that got away, I'd guess."

"What are their names, Tobe?"

"Huh? I don't know them."

"I say you do," Slocum said. "I say you know a whole hell of a lot about everything that's been going on around here lately, and I say it's time you started talking."

"Hey. You're— You're all wrong about that."

"You killed Ziggie, you little shit," Slocum said. "He never sent you back to the ranch by yourself. You started back together, and you dropped back behind him and shot him in the back. Just before you done that, he said that

Charlie Dode was robbing him blind. Remember that?"

Tobe looked at Marla. Then he looked at Rance. He saw no help in their faces. Both returned hard, cold stares. Neither spoke. He looked back at Slocum.

"Ziggie fired you," he said. "You killed him on accounta that."

"No one buys that bullshit anymore, Tobe," said Slocum. "You thought you killed Burl Johnson too, didn't you? But Burl ain't dead. He don't buy that shit anymore. You see, Tobe, whenever you shot poor old Ziggie in the back, you had a witness. You didn't know that did you? Or maybe you did know it, and that's how come you killed him too. Myron watched the whole thing. How do you think I know what Ziggie said to you before you killed him?"

"Why, I—"

"Yeah, Tobe," said Marla, "how'd Slocum know that?"

"Well, I—I don't know how he knowed that. I mean, he never knowed any such a thing on accounta Ziggie never said nothing like that. Slocum's making up that whole damn story. He's making it all up."

"Prove it, Tobe," Slocum said.

"What?"

"Prove it."

"I—I ain't drawing on you, Slocum. I got better sense than that."

"What's wrong, Tobe? You don't like killing a man when he's looking at you? I'll turn around."

Slocum turned his back on Tobe. He stood there with his hands crossed over his chest.

"You'll never have a better chance," he said. "Go on. Kill me if you got the guts for it."

"Rance?" said Tobe.

Then Slocum heard a movement behind him. He went for his Colt, stepped to one side and whirled all in one swift motion. But when his Colt was up, cocked, and leveled, he heard a roar, and he saw Tobe jerk, saw the hole appear in Tobe's chest, watched as Tobe's face took on a stupid expression, and as his gun hand went limp. Tobe stood for a moment, weaving back and forth. "Rance, you—" Then his knees buckled, and he dropped hard. He pitched forward on his face. He was dead.

Slocum turned his head to see Marla with the Colt in her hand and a cold expression on her otherwise beautiful face. He took a deep breath and let it out in a sigh. He holstered his Colt. Then he shook his head slowly.

"I thought you were looking for proof, lady," he said.

"We had proof enough," said Marla. "Let's get these poor boys buried."

9

On the long and slow ride back to the ranch with the bawling cattle dragging along, Slocum noticed that Marla and Rance were keeping pretty close together, and they talked low so that no one else could hear what they were saying. In turn, Slocum scowled his way through the cattle drive, not speaking unless he was spoken to and then answering in as few words as possible. When they bedded down on the second night on the trail, he asked himself what was wrong with him. Marla was a damn good-looking woman, but she didn't mean anything to him. Not really.

Was he jealous of Rance simply because he had dreamt a dream? That would be stupid. It had been a really sultry dream at that, and thinking back on it, Slocum realized that it had been most realistic. Even now, he recalled it almost as if it had really happened. He went to sleep that night with mixed feelings, with the delight of the events of the dream, and with the disgust of the company Marla and Rance were keeping. As he was falling asleep, he was trying to conjure up fresh images such as the ones of the night before, but it didn't work. Instead, he dreamed of bawling cows, mending fences, and bucking broncs.

When they at last arrived back at the ranch, Slocum ate his supper, then saddled the Appaloosa. As he was mounting up, Rance happened by. "Going somewhere, Slocum?" Rance asked. "Thought I'd spy around out to the mine," Slocum said, his voice low and grumpy. "Be careful," Rance advised. Slocum did not bother answering that last remark. He kicked up his big horse and they rode away fast. He kept up the pace until they were well out of sight. Then he slowed down and moved on toward the mine at a more leisurely speed.

When he reached the place where old Ziggie had been killed, he stopped and looked around. The landscape changed near the mine. The flat prairie gradually grew a little more rolling, and then suddenly mountains rose up. The far edge of the ranch just reached into the mountains, just enough to take in the silver mine. The sun was almost down, and Slocum did not want to ride too close in until the night was full dark. Up on the side of the mountain, Charlie Dode or any of his henchmen could see well out onto the prairie. He sat there studying his surroundings.

If he were to turn off the road to his left, he could ride up into the mountains a good distance south of the mine. Then he might be able to find a way up onto the mountainside where he would have that advantage, a spot where he could watch the road that ran to and from the mine. He decided to take that chance, and he turned the Appaloosa. He rode slow and easy, moving across open range in the darkness.

Reaching the base of the mountain, he turned and moved back toward the mine. At one point, he stopped his horse and sat to listen. He could hear the sound of water running. It was getting darker. The sun was just peeking over the western edge of the horizon. He moved slowly, looking carefully at the rocky side of the mountain, and then he saw the water running out of the rock. There was good grass down on the flat, and now he had found fresh water.

He looked at the side of the mountain again, studying for a way up. Thinking that he had found one, he dismounted and unsaddled the Appaloosa. He knew the big horse would stay close waiting for his return. He patted it and spoke to it softly. Then he headed for the location he had already scoped out. He started climbing. It wasn't a difficult climb, and soon he was up perhaps eighty feet and settled into a snug declivity in the side of the rock. He could see the road well from this vantage point. He took out a cigar and lit it. Then he leaned back into the rock to wait and watch.

Slocum's view of the mine was not good, but he could tell that there were lights on. Several hours had passed before he felt safe enough to go back down for his horse and ride in closer for a better view. Then he saw the movement. He squinted at it, but he couldn't really tell what was going on. But something was happening in the wee hours, and that was enough to make him suspicious. He sat watching for a while. Then he saw the wagon roll out onto the road. He knew what was happening then. There was no legitimate reason for a wagon to move out in the middle of the night. It was just as he suspected. They were taking the ore out in secret.

He sat still for a while, allowing the wagon to move slowly on down the road. Then he started on its trail. He stayed well back so he would not be spotted, and he rode away the rest of the night in that manner. When the sun came up at last, he managed to get close enough to see that the wagon had two men in it. He fell back again out of sight.

The wagon moved along at what seemed like a snail's pace to Slocum. He kept his distance. He knew that he could have taken the two men easily, but that was not his purpose. He wanted to find out where they were taking the stuff. In a few more miles, the wagon stopped, and the men built a small fire and prepared themselves a meal. Slocum waited impatiently. They did not move. When they finished their meal, they bedded down.

"Damn," Slocum snarled. Still, he waited. He had not slept either, but he could not afford to allow himself to drop off. They might leave again. He waited them out, and when they got up at last and started moving again, he followed them. He moved along slowly behind them all that day, and when night fell again, they stopped. Slocum decided that they were stopping for the night this time, so he made himself a camp and slept.

He was up early the next morning, and he rode far enough ahead to check on them. They were just getting ready to leave. He held back until they were rolling again. Then he moved after them. In a few miles they passed a sign that indicated a town was just ahead. It was called "Complacency." Slocum believed that they had already ridden out of the Territory at some point, but he wasn't sure. Well, maybe Complacency was their destination. He rode on easy.

Soon traffic appeared on the road, and then, as Slocum moved on into Complacency, he was surprised to find that it was a fairly busy little place. It didn't take him long to spot where the two men had pulled up with the wagon. The wagon was stopped just in front of an office that had several signs on its front: Assayer, Gold and Silver Bought Here, Register Claims, and others. One of the men still sat on the wagon seat, a rifle across his knees. Slocum rode on by and stopped in front of the saloon. It was not open. He hitched the Appaloosa at the rail there anyway, dismounted, and went up onto the board sidewalk to lounge.

In just a few minutes, he saw the other man come back out and point to a large barn door in the building next door. The man on the wagon seat put down his rifle, took up the reins and drove the wagon into the building. Slocum watched for another half hour at least until the wagon came back out. It had been unloaded. The two men walked across the street to a café and went inside. Slocum figured that they were going for breakfast, so he knew it would be a wait. He looked for a different eating place, and he found it across the street from the one the mine thieves had found. He went in and took a seat at a table by the front window where he could watch the front door of the other café. He ordered steak and eggs and coffee and sat there watching.

He was halfway through his breakfast when he saw them come out again. He watched through the window as they walked back over to their waiting wagon, climbed in and headed out of town in the direction they had come from. Slocum thought a moment, then resumed his breakfast. When he finished, he had one last cup of coffee. Then he paid for his meal and left. He walked down to the place where the two men had unloaded, and he went into the office. A man behind a counter looked up.

"Can I help you?" he asked.

"I want to know about those two men who just left here," Slocum said.

"Just a minute," the man said. He turned and walked to a side door, opened it and whispered to another man in the other room, "Go get the sheriff." Then he walked back to his spot behind the counter. "Now just what would you like to know?"

"I already know they dumped off a load of silver ore here," Slocum said. "Did they sell it?"

"Mister, you ought to know I can't answer questions like that."

"Look here," said Slocum, "I work for the Circle Z Ranch over near Rascality. That load of ore came off the Circle Z mine. There's been some ore disappearing, unaccounted for. I followed those boys over here from the mine to check up on them. They left the mine in the middle of the night."

"How do I know that? What if you're just looking to rob somebody and you want to know if they got paid? I can't take your word for it you work for ole Ziggie."

"So you know Ziggie?"

"Knowed him for years."

"Well, he's dead," said Slocum. "They killed him 'cause he suspected them of robbing him. Now his daughter's in charge, and I'm working for her."

The door opened and a man with a badge on his shirt stepped in. He was a big man with a handlebar mustache. He shut the door behind himself, hitched his pants up by the waist, and said, "Trouble, Benny?"

"Not much, Mac," said the man behind the counter. "This fella here just come in and started in to asking all kinds a questions about two of old Ziggie's miners. They just left here, and then this one come in with his questions. I told him I can't answer questions like that, but he claims that

Ziggie's been killed, and he's working for Ziggie's daughter."

"I ain't heard nothing about ole Ziggie getting himself killed," the sheriff said.

"Sometimes news travels slow," Slocum said.

"Yeah? And sometimes crooks make up stories."

Slocum hesitated. He looked from the sheriff to Benny and back again. Then he said, "Hell, I can see I ain't getting no place here. I'll just ride on out of town."

The sheriff's gun was out fast, leveled at Slocum's belly. "And ride after them two, I reckon," he said. He held out his left hand and wiggled his fingers. "Take off the gun belt," he said.

"Now, wait a minute—"

"Take it off."

Slocum unbuckled the belt and handed it to the sheriff.

"Now, come along with me," the sheriff said, holstering his own revolver. Slocum walked with the sheriff down the street to the jailhouse and went inside. The sheriff dropped Slocum's gun belt on his desk as he walked on around it to take his seat. He gestured toward another chair, and Slocum sat down.

"Now, suppose you tell me all about this business," the sheriff said.

"Those two men are part of a scheme to ruin the Circle Z," Slocum said. "I've been hired by Miss Marla to stop them. If they sold that load of ore just a while ago, I can guarantee you that Miss Marla will never hear about it, and the money they got won't find its way into her bank account neither."

"Hold it," the sheriff said. "I don't know nothing about no Miss Marla. You said something a while ago about old Ziggie getting himself killed. Let's start right there."

Slocum sighed. "Ziggie rode out to the mine to quiz up his foreman out there, and he never came back," he said. "They found him on the road with a bullet in his back. Marla's his daughter. She's taken over the place, and she hired me to find out what's going on. That's how come I followed those two over here from the mine when they left out two nights ago in the middle of the night."

"Why would they do a fool thing like that?" the sheriff asked.

"You figure it out," said Slocum. "They just pulled into town a little while ago."

"And you claim you been following them all that time?"

"I did."

"What for?"

"I wanted to find out where they were going and what they were going to do with the ore. Damn it, Sheriff—"

The sheriff rubbed his chin. "It's like ole Benny said. You could be anyone. You could be planning to rob them two."

"Damn it, Sheriff, time's wasting. They're getting away with Marla's money."

"You just calm down. I got to check up on your story."

"How the hell're you going to check up on it?"

"I'll send a wire over to Rascality."

"Damn it, that could take two days or more."

"It don't take no time at all for a wire to go through. You're in an all fired hurry, ain't you? Afraid them two are going to get away from you?"

"Marla's out at the ranch," Slocum said. "She won't get that wire right when it comes in."

"Well, she'll get it soon enough," the sheriff said. He took a piece of paper and a pencil out of a desk drawer and started writing. Then he got up and walked to the door. He opened the door, waited a minute or so, then yelled, "Hey, Scampy. Come over here." Slocum sat in the chair waiting. Soon he heard another voice, and then the sheriff said, "Take this over to the telegraph office and tell Wiley to send it for me. Tell him to bring the answer back over here to me soon as he gets it. Okay?"

"Yes, sir."

The sheriff walked back over to his desk and sat down again. He opened another desk drawer and brought out a bottle and two glasses. He poured them both full.

"Might as well enjoy your wait," he said.

Slocum sighed again. He stood up to reach for the glass. "Might as well," he said. He picked up the glass and sat down again. Then he took a sip.

"Good whiskey, ain't it?" the sheriff said.

"It's good," said Slocum.

"What's your name?"

"John Slocum."

"John Slocum. Seems I heard that name somewhere before. What do you do, John Slocum?"

"I told you that already. You trying to slip me up? I'm working for Marla Ziglinsky. She hired me to find out what's been going on around the Circle Z."

"You ain't been working for Marla Ziglinsky very long," the sheriff said. "You said Ziggie got shot, and then she hired you. What the hell was you doing before that?"

"I'd been busting broncs for ole Ziggie, but he fired me. Whenever Marla hired me, I was out of a job."

"How come ole Ziggie to fire your ass?"

"That ain't got nothing to do with all this."

"Maybe it ain't and maybe it does. How come?"

"I got in a fight with another hand over my horse," Slocum said. "Ziggie said that whenever I hired on with him, so did my horse. I didn't agree with that."

"Say, I just now recollect where I heard of you from. You killed ole Aaron Parsons, didn't you? The one they called One Shot?"

"I did that."

"Yeah. Slocum. Hell, yes, I remember that now. That was up in Harleyville."

"Near there."

"That was quite a story. Quite a story. They said you was a lawman at the time."

"Just briefly," said Slocum. "I don't like that story spread around. I took that badge off soon as I got the job done."

The sheriff laughed. "I'll be damned. Ole Slocum. Slocum himself. What killed ole One Shot. Well, listen, Slocum, I can't be sitting here all day like this. Why don't you just make yourself comfortable in that there cell while we wait for an answer to my wire?"

"Am I under arrest?"

"No. Hell no. What for? You're just a guest here is all. Take that glass and that bottle with you. Go on now."

Slocum stood up with his glass, and he grabbed the bottle off the top of the sheriff's desk. Then he walked into the cell. He wasn't too surprised when the sheriff slammed the door and locked it. He sat on the edge of the cot and poured himself another drink.

"Don't worry, Slocum," the sheriff said. "I'll be back just as soon as I get my answer to that there wire. If you're telling the truth, you'll be out and on your way."

"Yeah, thanks a lot," Slocum said, and he took a long slug of whiskey as the sheriff walked out the front door and disappeared. Slocum thought that his streak of shitty luck was sure holding.

10

Rance and Marla were in the living room of the big ranch house waiting impatiently for some word from Slocum. They were also waiting for Doc to come back out of the bedroom and give them some word about Burl Johnson. Doc had ordered a cup of coffee and a bowl of chicken broth for the patient. He had not allowed anyone to come into the room as yet though, except for his nurse, Hettie. Burl Johnson had finally come to, and Doc wanted to make sure that the sheriff did not starve to death. He wanted him fed a little bit, and he did not want him bothered, not for a while yet.

Marla was pacing the floor when the doc at last came out of the bedroom and shut the door behind himself. She turned and faced Doc, anxious. "He's sleeping now," Doc said.

"Did he say anything about what happened to him out there?" Marla asked.

"Nope. I never asked him, and I don't want you or anyone else bothering him either. He's lucky he even came out of that. He needs his rest."

"How soon will he be able to talk?" asked Rance.

"I'll let you know," said the doc. "Just hold your horses. Anyhow, I've got a baby to deliver. I'll be back around early in the morning. Like I said, you stay out of there till I say different. Hettie can take care of whatever might come up."

"Okay, Doc," Rance said.

"Yeah," said Marla. "Thanks."

Doc put on his hat and left the room by the front door. "Good night," he said, shutting the door behind himself.

"I wonder what's keeping Slocum," Marla said.

"What?" said Rance.

"Slocum," she said. "I wonder what's keeping him. He's been gone now for, what, three days? What could be keeping him?"

"He said he was going out to keep an eye on the mine," said Rance.

"Yeah. I know. I wonder what's keeping him."

"Maybe nothing's happened. Maybe he's still watching."

"Well, I don't like it."

"You think something could've gone wrong out there?"

"I think Slocum can handle himself all right," Marla said. "It's just all this waiting is getting to me, I guess."

"You don't think he could've taken off, do you?"

"You mean run out on me? No. I don't think so."

"Maybe Slocum was right all along," Rance said.

"How do you mean?"

"Well, maybe Dode and them was sneaking stuff out at night. Maybe he seen them and followed along. No telling how far away they're taking it."

Marla walked over to Rance and put her hands on his shoulders. She sighed. "Oh, Rance, you're probably right about that. I just wish I knew, that's all."

She laid her head against Rance's chest. Rance put his arms around her and held her close.

"Everything's going to be all right, Marla," he said. "You'll see."

"Rance," she said, "right now, before Hettie comes out of the room, go to my room and wait for me there. Please."

"All right, Marla," he said. He let her go and walked quickly down the hallway and turned into her bedroom, shutting the door behind himself. Marla paced the floor some more. She went to the liquor cabinet and poured herself a drink. She was sipping the whiskey when Hettie came out of the bedroom.

"Hello, Hettie," Marla said. "Is Burl still sleeping?"

"Yes," said Hettie. "I expect he'll sleep all night, but I'll be in the room with him, just in case."

"Do you need anything?"

"I was just going to the kitchen to make some coffee, if that's all right."

"Of course it's all right, but you don't have to make any. There's almost a full fresh pot. Just help yourself."

"Thanks."

"Hettie," said Marla. "I'm going on to bed. I'll see you in the morning."

"All right," Hettie said. "Good night."

"Good night."

Hettie went on into the kitchen, and Marla took an extra glass and hurried on down to her own room at the end of the hallway. She opened the door and stepped inside, closing the door again behind herself. Rance stood up from the chair in which he had been sitting. Marla walked over to him and handed him the extra glass. Then she poured it full.

"Thanks," he said, and he took a sip.

Marla took a sip out of her own glass, then put the bottle and glass on the table beside her bed. She turned back the covers, then turned to face Rance. She sat on the edge of the bed and pulled off her boots. Then she stood and unfastened her jeans and wriggled out of them. Rance put his glass down and started climbing out of his own clothes. Marla was stripped first, and she crawled into the bed. When Rance was naked, he blew out the light and crawled in beside her. He crawled into her open arms. His right hand found her left breast in the darkness, and he squeezed it as his lips searched for hers. Their lips met at last, and they kissed, at first tenderly, gently, then harder. Soon they parted their lips, and their tongues began to probe into each other's mouths.

Rance slipped his right hand off the lovely tit and ran it down her belly until he found the mound of wet pubic hair. He stroked until his finger slipped into the juicy hole. "Um," she moaned. "Oh." She moved her left hand down to his crotch and gripped his already hard and throbbing rod. She squeezed it tight as it tried to buck in her hand. Then she pulled her lips away from his and moved them close to his ear. "Slip that inside me," she whispered.

She spread her legs wide as Rance moved on top of her, and she guided the hungry cock to the waiting hole. "There," she said. "There." Rance shoved, and his cock slipped in. He drove it deep, as she thrust forward with her hips. "Ah," said Rance. "Ah, that's good."

"Give it to me, Rance," she said.

Rance began to pump, slowly at first, then harder and faster. Marla's upward thrusts kept up the same rhythm. She reached around him, gripping a check of his ass with each hand. "Come on," she said. "Give it to me. Give it to me." Rance drove as hard and fast as he could. Sweat popped out on his forehead and ran down his face, dripping off onto her round and wriggling breasts.

"Oh, oh, oh, Rance," she said.

She dug her nails into his butt, and he ground his teeth to keep from crying out loud. "Damn," he said through clenched teeth. "Oh, goddamn." Then he exploded into her depths. "Ah. Oh." He spurted again and again. At last he stopped, and he lay still, his weight pressing down on her body. She still wiggled, still thrust. Obviously, she was not yet satisfied. Rance lay still panting for another minute or so, and then he pulled out and backed down, trailing his tongue along her belly, searching until he found just the right spot. Then he began to lap.

Marla went wild. She bucked and humped, and Rance had to hang onto her waist with both hands to keep from being tossed aside. Even so, he kept up his magic tongue work, her legs wrapped around his head. "Ah," she screamed and rolled over onto her belly, dragging Rance along with her. He was on his back now, and she was humping his face, pressing him hard into the mattress beneath them. He was having trouble catching his breath. He hoped that he could keep it up long enough to satisfy her lust. At last she cried out, "God.

That's enough. Stop it. Stop it. I can't stand any more."

She quit her thrusting and rolled off him onto her back. She lay there gasping for breath. Rance did not move. He couldn't. He stayed right where she left him, lying on the sticky, wet sheet, his face smeared with her cunt juice. Then she said, "You'd better go out the window. I wouldn't want anyone to see you leave my bedroom."

Doc was true to his word. He was pounding on the door early in the morning. Hettie was the first one to the door to let him in. "Any change?" he asked her.

"I think he's just trying to wake up," she said. Together they walked into the bedroom. Just about then, Marla came out of her room, dressed and ready to start the day. She saw the door to the other bedroom shut, and she walked to the front window to look out and see Doc's buggy. She went on into the kitchen to put on a fresh pot of coffee and start some breakfast. She had put some bacon on to fry when she heard the knock at the door. She hurried to the front door and opened it to let Rance in.

"Good morning," he said.

"Come on in, Rance. Doc's in there with Burl. I'm cooking breakfast."

Rance followed her to the kitchen where she put him right to work. In a few minutes, they had the table spread with bacon, eggs, biscuits, and gravy. Doc came out of the bedroom.

"Doc," Marla said, "sit down and have some breakfast with us."

Doc put down his bag and walked over to the table. "Don't mind if I do," he said. "It's been a spell since I had anything to eat."

Hettie came into the big room then, and Doc said to her, "Fix our patient a plate, Hettie. I think he can take it now. And fix one for yourself."

"All right, Doc," she said. She fixed two modest plates and carried them back into the bedroom. Doc piled his own plate high.

"Doc?" said Marla.

"Um?"

"Does that mean that Burl can be questioned now about what happened out there?"

"I reckon he can," said Doc, "but let's wait till he's had his breakfast. Okay?"

"Sure."

Hettie came back for two cups of coffee and then went back into the bedroom. When they had all finished eating, Marla got up and poured more coffee around the table. She was impatient, and it showed. Finally, Hettie came back out again. She was carrying the plates and the cups. She put the plates in the kitchen, and came out again.

"Doc," she said, "Burl wants another cup of coffee. Is it all right?"

"Sure," said Doc. "He can have all the coffee he wants. Did he get enough to eat?"

"Yes," said Hettie. "He said so."

She poured the coffee and went back into the room. Doc got up and followed her. In another minute, he came back out.

"It's all right now," he said, "if you want to come in."

Marla was up and in the room in a hurry, and Rance was just a short ways behind. Burl smiled weakly when he saw them.

"How you doing, Burl?" asked Rance.

"I guess I'm doing all right," Burl said, "considering."

"Burl," said Marla, "there's something we got to ask you."

"I'm listening."

"What happened to you out there?"

"Damned if I know," said Burl. "Slocum's the one who can answer that. He was with me."

"He brought you in here to us," Marla said.

"I reckon I owe him my life then."

"Yeah, but before that. What's the last thing you remember?"

"Um. Well, me and ole Slocum was at a camp. See, he set up an ambush for me. Got the drop on me. Then we talked a spell, and he gave me back my gun and put his away. We were just talking, you know. He offered me a cigar. I was reaching for it. That's the last I recall."

"Then he couldn't have shot you?"

"Slocum? Hell no. I mean, he could have. Easy. If he'd a wanted to. But he never done it. No way. I was looking right at him."

"So you got no idea who done it?" asked Rance.

"Nothing I could take to court," said Burl. "I got my suspicions."

"Tobe?"

"You said it. Say, where is Slocum right now?"

"Wish I knew," said Marla.

"He went out to watch the mine two nights ago," Rance said. "We ain't heard from him since."

Burl wrinkled his brow. "Maybe he's found something to watch out there," he said. "I hope so."

"Burl," said Rance, "just what is Slocum's status with you now?"

"Far as I'm concerned," Burl said, "Slocum's free and clear. Hell, I ain't even going to charge him with busting my head to get out of jail."

"Well, now—"

"Well, now, nothing," said Doc. "That's enough for now. You two get on out of here. Go on now. Burl's got to rest."

Rance and Marla left the room, and in another few minutes, Doc came out again. He walked up to Marla, digging into his pocket for a piece of paper, which he handed her.

"I almost forgot," he said. "Arnold asked me to bring this out here to you. It just came in this morning."

Back in the jail in Complacency, Slocum was stretched out on the cot when the sheriff brought him his breakfast. He thought about trying to break out of jail as he had done in Rascality, but then he considered the amount of trouble he had caused himself with that one, so he just sat still. This stupid sheriff had nothing with which to charge him anyway. He was just inconveniencing him a little.

"You get an answer to that wire?" he asked.

"Not yet," said the sheriff. "You just eat your breakfast and be patient. I'll get one directly."

Slocum sipped at the coffee. The sheriff left him alone again to finish his meal. It was mid-morning before he returned. This time Slocum did not bother asking, but the sheriff walked over to the cell door and opened it. Slocum looked up at him.

"Well, come on out," the sheriff said.

"I was just getting comfortable," Slocum said.

"Come on," the sheriff said.

Slocum stood up and ambled out. The sheriff walked over to the desk, picked up Slocum's gun belt and held it out to him. Slocum took it and strapped it on.

"I take it you got your answer," he said.

"Just now. Ziggie's dead all right. His daughter Marla is in charge of the ranch. She says you're working for her. Backed you up all the way. You can ride on out anytime you're a mind to."

"Thanks a lot, Sheriff," Slocum said. "You know, those two thieving bastards I followed here have got a hell of a long head start on me now with their stolen money."

"Well now, if you're lucky, all they done was just to ride back to the mine with it. You just head on back there and find out before you go placing any blame anywhere. A man in my position has got to be mighty careful what he does. I got to check everything out, you know."

"Shit," Slocum said, walking out the door.

He thought about riding hard to try to catch them before they got back to the mine. After all, they were driving a wagon, and he was on his big Appaloosa, but then, it didn't seem worth running his horse to death. Chances were the damned sheriff was right. They just took the money back to the mine, or wherever it was that ole Dode was stashing it. They hadn't been bothered for a few days, so they were probably pretty confident that everything was okay. He decided that he'd just ride on back to the ranch and report what he'd discovered to Marla. They could figure out what to do from there. He went to the store for some trail provisions so that he wouldn't starve again along the way, and then he headed out at an easy pace.

11

Slocum rode slowly up to the big ranch house, and Marla stepped out onto the porch to meet him. He swung heavily down out of the saddle, slapped the reins around the hitch rail, and walked up the steps of the porch. "Howdy," he said.

"Where've you been?"

"Oh, I took a little ride out of the territory over to a little town called Complacency. It was right interesting."

It was the middle of the day, a little early, but Slocum looked like he could use it, so Marla offered him a drink. "I don't mind," he said. He followed her inside, and she poured him a glass full of good, brown whiskey. He took a sip, and then he sat down. Marla took a chair opposite him.

"So?" she said. "You going to tell me about it?"

"I followed a wagon out of the mine," he said. "It left out in the middle of the night. Followed it for two days to this place called Complacency. I watched while they unloaded. Then I went to ask some questions and got myself throwed in jail. Had to sit there and wait for your answer to the sheriff's wire."

"That's it?"

"That's it. Well, after you answered the wire, I got some answers to my questions. They're selling ore, all right, by the wagon load. Remember that safe out at the mine office? I betcha it's full of your money."

99

"Damn," Marla said. "Well, what now?"

"You're the boss," Slocum said.

"Well, shit, Slocum," she said, "just pretend like you're the boss for a change and tell me what the hell you'd do?"

"I'd ride out there and kill some folks," he said, "if I was the boss."

"I tend to agree with you, but we'll talk it over with Rance and with, well, come along with me. I got something to show you."

Slocum stood up and followed Marla into the extra bedroom where they found Sheriff Burl Johnson sitting up in bed. Johnson grinned wide at the sight of Slocum and extended a hand. Slocum took his hand. "Well, I'll be damned," he said. "You're looking some better than you was last time I saw you."

"I owe it to you, Slocum," Johnson said.

"Hell, I had to look out for you. Far as I knew, you were the only person on my side at the time."

"Well, yeah. I'm a slow learner sometimes, but I do come around. Say, where the hell you been? I've been awake for a couple of days now."

Slocum told Johnson the tale of the wagon load of ore and how he followed it to Complacency.

"I asked him what he'd do if he was the boss," Marla said, "and he said he'd go over there and kill some folks. I agree with him. What do you say?"

"Well, now, I'm a lawman. You know I can't agree with that."

"That's just the point, Burl," Marla snapped. "You are the law in these parts, and look at you. We just told you what's been going on. What the hell are you going to do about it?"

"I'll tell you what I'd do if I was up and around," Johnson said. "I'd ride out there and arrest Charlie Dode and charge him with theft or something. Then there'd be a trial, and then—"

"Dode wouldn't just ride in with you quiet-like," Slocum said.

"Well, I'd have made the attempt."

"Then you'd kill him."

"If I had to."

"Okay, so that's what you'd do if you was up and around," Marla said, "but you ain't. So what the hell am I supposed to do? Let Charlie Dode keep on robbing me blind while you lay there and heal up?"

"Stop sounding like your daddy," said Johnson. "I have an idea, if you'll listen to it."

"All right," she said. "I'm listening."

"We want to keep this all legal and aboveboard," Johnson said. "How many men does Dode have working at the mine?"

"He's got a crew of a dozen men," Marla said.

"Do you know how many are in on this scheme with him?"

"My guess would be all of them," Slocum said. "They have to know he's taking those wagons out in the middle of the night. They have to know that Ziggie suspected Dode of stealing from him. They've all got to be in on it."

"I checked the books," Marla said. "Daddy let Charlie hire all the men out there."

"All right," Johnson said. "Why don't you round up as many of your cowhands as are willing and can handle a gun? Bring them in here, and I'll appoint them all special deputies. But there's one hitch."

"What is it?"

"Slocum here has got to agree to be one of them, and he's in charge."

"Damn," said Slocum. "I hate to get roped into wearing a badge."

"You won't have to wear a badge," Johnson said, "but you will be a deputy. What do you say?"

"I'll go for it," Marla said.

"All right," Slocum grumbled.

"Wait a minute," said Johnson. "If we do this, it's got to be done my way. I'll swear in all the deputies and write up a paper on it. Then I'll fill out an arrest warrant. I'll give you the warrant, Slocum, and you take the whole damn posse to the mine and arrest Charlie Dode and the whole damn crew. If they resist, well, then, you do what you have to do."

Marla looked anxiously at Slocum. "Well?" she said.

"All right," Slocum said. "We'll do it your way."

"Round up your crew then," Johnson said, "and bring some paper and a pen."

In short order, six cowhands, Rance, and Slocum were sworn in. Johnson wrote up the paper, and then he wrote on another sheet the warrant for the arrest of Charlie Dode and the entire mine crew. He handed the warrant to Slocum, who folded it and tucked it away in a pocket.

"All right, Slocum," Johnson said, "it's all in your hands now."

"Thanks a lot," Slocum said. "Come on, boys. We got some planning to do."

Rance and the six cowhands followed Slocum out onto the porch. Slocum took the hat off his head and slapped his leg with it. He stood staring off in the direction of the mine. "Well, Slocum?" Rance said.

"Well, shut up and give me some time to think," Slocum said. "This thing come on me kinda sudden-like."

"I say we just ride out there and start shooting," Rance said.

"That's likely how come you ain't in charge," said Slocum. "You sound like your ole pal Tobe."

"This is different," said Rance. "You got the goods on Dode and them. Tobe shot poor ole Myron for no reason, and he blamed you real fast for killing Ziggie too."

"I seem to recall you blaming me for killing Ziggie," Slocum said.

"Well, yeah, I was wrong about that."

"I could be wrong about Charlie Dode too. That's how come Johnson told me to arrest him. If he comes along without no fight, well, good for him. He can get a trial."

"All right. I ain't arguing no more. What do you want to do?"

Rance rankled Slocum, but Slocum was afraid that it was all because of Marla. That annoyed him. He told himself once again that Marla was nothing to him. He'd only known her for a short while. Rance had likely known her for years. If Rance was thinking of marriage, he was likely thinking that he had a pretty good stake in the Circle Z too, having been foreman for however long. In fact, Slocum told himself, it was most likely a pretty good match at that. Marla was a fairly tough gal, but she couldn't really run the Circle Z by herself. Partnering up with old Rance was probably the smartest thing she could do under the circumstances. He told himself that, but he still didn't like it. There was just something about Rance that pissed him off.

"Rance," he said, calming himself down, "boys, let's all take the rest of the day to get ourselves ready for a big fight. We might not have one, but likely we will. So we want to be ready for it. Rance, has the ranch got a good store of ammunition?"

"We got plenty," Rance said.

"I want every man to be well supplied. If you ain't got enough of your own, see Rance and get some more. Okay?"

"Sure," Rance said.

"Take your side arm and a rifle with you and plenty of shells for both of them. Check your weapons over real good. Other than that, just take it easy and get a good night's sleep. In the morning, be ready to ride with the daylight. We'll meet right over at the corral. Any questions?"

"What're we going to do when we get to the mine?" Rance asked.

"You ain't going to do nothing," said Slocum, "except keep alert. I'll holler up at Dode and tell him what the deal is and that he's under arrest. If him and the others come out, we'll just take them in to jail. That's all."

"And if they don't?"

"Let them shoot first," Slocum said. "But if they start it, then cut loose."

The posse broke up then, and Slocum walked over to the hitch rail where his big Appaloosa stood patiently waiting for him. He swung up into the saddle and turned the horse toward the road.

"Hey, Slocum," Rance called out. "Where you headed?"

"I'll see you in the morning," Slocum answered. He didn't really want anyone to know where he was going, especially not Rance. Out at the road, he turned toward Rascality. It was still early in the afternoon, and he rode easy. It was early evening by the time he reached town, and he pulled up in front of the livery stable. He told the man there to take good care of his horse, and he walked on over to the Hognose Saloon. He walked inside and up to the bar where he ordered a bottle and two glasses. He paid for them, picked them up and turned to look around. He spotted Rowdy trying to drum up some business with a reluctant cowhand, and he walked over, took her by the arm, and said, "Come on with me, Rowdy."

"Hey," she protested, but she went along.

"He couldn't make up his mind nohow," said Slocum. He led Rowdy to the stairs and started climbing. "I didn't make a good showing with you the last time I was here," he said. "I don't like to leave a bad impression."

"Hey, you don't have to prove nothing to me," Rowdy said.

"I mean to anyhow."

At the top of the stairs, Slocum hesitated. "Which room?" he asked. "I wasn't in much shape to recall from last time."

"Look, mister—"

"The name's Slocum. Which room?"

"Right there," she said.

Slocum dragged her to the room, opened the door, and dragged her through it. He shut the door and slung her toward the bed. Then he grabbed a chair and jammed it up under the doorknob. Rowdy sat on the edge of the bed staring at Slocum as he unbuckled his gun belt. He hung the rig on a peg on the wall, then put his hat on one next to it. He pulled off his shirt and tossed it on the chair. Then he walked to the bed to sit down beside Rowdy. He pulled off his boots, and then stood up to take off his jeans. As he did, he looked down at her.

"Well?" he said.

Rowdy started undoing her bodice, but Slocum was stripped before her, and he began pulling her clothes off. He had her naked too in another moment, and he put her on the bed on her hands and knees with her round ass cheeks poking out toward him. He stood on the floor behind her, his tool ready for action, and he moved in and slid himself into her sheath. He wasted no time. He banged hard into her again and again, his body slapping against her ass. He could see her titties shake where they were hanging down beneath her. "Oh, oh, oh," she said.

Slocum felt the pressure building up in his heavy balls, but he wasn't ready to shoot into her. He pulled out and climbed up onto the bed, lying down on his back. He grabbed Rowdy and pulled her onto him. "Oh, God," she said, straddling his waist. She took hold of his throbbing rod and guided it back into the now slimy slit. Then she sat down easy until the swollen cock was all the way inside her.

"Oh, yes," she said, beginning to rock back and forth, sliding along his belly and upper thighs in their mingling sweat. She smiled with the pleasure as she moved faster and faster, moaning out loud as she did. "Oh, fuck," she said. "Fuck." Slocum could feel her juices running out and onto his belly, mixing with the sweat that was already there. Rowdy rocked back and forth furiously, sliding gloriously on the slippery mixture.

Suddenly she cried out in pleasure, and she rocked more slowly for a few more strokes before she stopped altogether. She threw back her head and sucked in deep breaths. Then she lowered her head to look down at Slocum. She fell forward, mashing her breasts against his chest, and she kissed him full on the mouth. At last she stopped. She looked him in the face. She was through. She knew that, but she also knew that he was not.

"What now?" she said.

"You guess," he said.

She raised her ass until his cock slipped free, and then she scooted backward like a crawdad until she was down between his legs, his rampant tool still standing, gleaming with the juices from her own cunt. She gripped it hard with her right hand, and she kissed it. Then she licked it up one side and down the other. At last, she opened her lips and sucked the head into her mouth. She slurped it out again, and then she did it again. At last, she gobbled up its entire length. Slocum thrust upward as she did.

Rowdy began sliding her head slowly up and down the length of Slocum's hard cock, cleaning it off as she did. She moved a bit faster and then faster yet as Slocum began a steady thrusting. "Um, um," she moaned. Her left hand found his balls and squeezed them.

Finally, Slocum could no longer contain himself. The pressure was too much. He could feel the explosion coming, and he no longer wanted to extend the time, even if he had been able. He gasped out loud as he spurted into her mouth. He thrust again and spurted again. And again. And again. At last he lay still. Rowdy squeezed his cock and sipped the last drop. Then she lay still stroking his now useless rod. At last she crawled up beside him and lay her head on his chest.

"The last time I was here," he said, "I told you I was too drunk."

"Well, you ain't too drunk now," she said.

"You want a drink?"

"I could use one."

Slocum got up and poured two drinks. He handed one to Rowdy, and then he crawled back beside her in the bed.

"Um," she said. "That's good."

"We'll have just this one drink," Slocum said. "Then I'll be ready to go again."

12

Slocum had one hell of a night, but in spite of it all, he was at the ranch house early the next morning ready to go. Like everyone else, he had gotten plenty of ammunition from the stores at the ranch. The big Appaloosa was saddled and ready for the ride, stamping around as if he knew there was excitement afoot. In just a short time, the six volunteer cowhands and Rance had joined Slocum there beside the corral. They were armed and mounted and anxious. Slocum rode out in front of them to address them.

"All right, boys," he said, "the first thing to remember is that, distasteful as it may be, we're all law officers right now. We got our orders direct from ole Burl in there. We don't shoot first. Remember that. I got to try to arrest Dode and them. If they resist, then we shoot, but not till then. Has everyone got that?"

"Everyone understands that, Slocum," Rance said. "Right, boys?"

"Yes, sir."

"That's right, Boss."

"All right then," said Slocum. "Let's ride."

He turned his horse toward the road to lead the way on out to the mine. As they moved along, Slocum kept thinking about Charlie Dode. He didn't really know any of Charlie's crew, but he could only assume that they worked with Dode and were in on the whole scheme. It could be a hell of a fight. On the other hand, if Dode had any good sense about him, he would ride on into town peaceful-like and take his chances with a judge. A good lawyer could drag a thing like this out for quite some time.

Slocum did not know what he hoped would happen. Part of him wanted to shoot Dode and any of his accomplices who were involved, but another part told him that any shooting would be dangerous to his small posse as well. The mine office was up on the side of the mountain looking down on the road. Slocum and the posse would be out in the open in full view, easy targets for anyone in the office to shoot down at with rifles. Their best chance was to catch Dode and the others by surprise. If the miners were caught at work in the mine, and Dode alone in the office, Slocum and the posse would have the distinct advantage. That's what Slocum was hoping for.

Back at the ranch house, Marla had watched the posse ride away and then gone back into the house. She prepared breakfast for herself, Hettie, and Johnson, and then she took the breakfasts in to Johnson and Hettie and ate her own by herself at the big table. She felt irritable. She had expected Rance to show up at the house last night, but he had never made an appearance. Now he was off with the posse, and she would not be able to question him about it until later. She managed to eat most of her breakfast, and she drank an extra cup of coffee before going in to check on Johnson and Hettie. She took the coffeepot with her and poured them each a fresh cup.

"How are you feeling this morning, Burl?" she asked, trying to get her mind off of Rance's neglect.

"Pretty good, Marla," Johnson said. "Considering everything. I know I'm lucky to be alive."

"I guess you are at that," Marla said.

"Oh, there's no question about it," Hettie said. "Doc told me that most men would've been killed by that bullet, and if Mr. Slocum hadn't got Burl here as fast as he did, we'd have lost Burl too. He's a lucky man all right."

"Well, I'm grateful to Slocum," said Johnson. "That's for sure. I owe him a life. And me starting out to try to slap him back in jail. He's an interesting fellow."

"That's for sure," Hettie agreed.

"Burl," Marla said, "what do you think will happen out there at the mine today?"

"It'll all depend on Charlie Dode," Johnson said. "Slocum will do what I told him to do. He'll try to arrest Charlie and the others. If they don't resist, it'll be all right."

"And if they do?"

"Then it'll be a big fight. It's hard to say how that'll come out. Charlie and them's got the advantage the way they're situated up there, but if Slocum takes them by surprise, well, that'll even things out some. They shouldn't be expecting any trouble up there, and I have a lot of confidence in Slocum."

"God," said Marla. "I hope our boys come out all right. I don't want to see anyone else killed."

"I just wish I could be out there with them," Johnson said.

"Now, you quit thinking like that," Hettie told him. "You're supposed to rest and relax."

"I got no choice about the resting part," Johnson said.

"It's the relaxing I'm talking about," said Hettie. "You just do your best to put this business out of your mind. Worrying over it won't change anything. When they get back, you'll find out what happened, and before that, it won't do any good to worry over it."

"That's easy to say," said Johnson.

"I'm sorry," Marla said. "I shouldn't have brought it up."

"It's not your fault," Johnson said. "I was already thinking about it before you came in."

"Well, try to relax, like Hettie says. Do either one of you need anything?"

Hettie and Johnson both said no, and so Marla excused herself and left the room. She still felt agitated, and she paced the floor some. Then she heard the sound of a buggy arriving in front of the house, and she went to the door and opened it to see Doc arriving. She greeted him and showed him into the house. He went right to the bedroom. Marla did not bother following him in there. She went into the kitchen and looked for something to do. There were only the breakfast dishes, so she cleaned them up. Then she went to the living room again and sat down behind the big desk.

Doc came out of the room and headed for the door, but Marla stopped him along his way. "How's he doing, Doc?" she asked.

"He's doing great," Doc said. "He'll be down for a time yet, but he'll come back most to normal. He's a tough man. Slocum got him back in time. I'm looking for a total recovery."

"That's great," she said. Doc left, and Marla once again was sitting behind the big desk looking for something to do to help pass the time. She had already gone over all the books. There was no more to be done there. She kept thinking about Rance. The son of a bitch, she thought. What's he trying to pull? He works for me. Does he think he can just show up in my bedroom when it's convenient for him? Goddamn him.

She thought about firing him to show him who was who and what was what, but a man not showing up for a secret rendezvous was really a poor excuse for that. He would likely tell everyone in the country about it too. No, there was nothing for it but to confront him and ask him why he had not shown. They'd had a clear understanding. He was supposed to be there. She kept telling herself to think of something else, but under the circumstances, she could think of nothing except Rance's failure to show, and the fight that was coming up at the mine. And thinking about the fight didn't help get her mind off Rance, because he was part of the posse. Damn it all.

She flipped back through the pages of one of Ziggie's old notebooks, and something caught her eye. "I told Rance I need a new mine foreman," the note said. "He recommended a man by the name of Charlie Dode. Sent Dode a note this morning." She stared at the words for another minute or two unbelieving. Charlie Dode was recommended by Rance? And then Charlie hired all his own miners. She told herself it didn't mean anything. She would ask Rance about it this evening. Likely, he just knew Dode in passing, had heard that he was a a good mine foreman. There would be some reasonable explanation. She was sure of it.

Slocum stopped his posse just beyond rifle range and studied the layout at the mine. He couldn't tell if anything was going on. He could not see any animals anywhere. He had a feeling that something was very wrong, but he did not want to take any unnecessary chances with the lives of the seven men who were with him. "Wait here," he told them, and he rode ahead slowly. Arriving close enough to shout up at the office, he stopped again.

"Hello," he called out. He waited. There was no answer. "Hello, in the mine."

"Who is it?"

"It's Slocum. I need to talk to you."

"You can talk from there."

"It ain't easy carrying on a conversation at this distance. Let me ride in closer."

"Ride slow, and stop when I tell you."

Slocum eased his Appaloosa forward, and when he had gone about half the distance to the mine, the voice called out again. "Hold it right there." He stopped.

"Who's that talking to me?" he called out. "Is Charlie Dode up there?"

"Never mind about Charlie Dode," said the voice. "Who are you and what do you want here? This here is private property."

"I'm Slocum. I work for the Circle Z, and I been made a deputy by Burl Johnson. I got seven more deputies with me. We're here to arrest Charlie Dode and everyone else who works in the mine. Come on down peaceful-like, and we'll ride into town. You'll get a fair trial."

"What's the charge?"

"Stealing from the mine," Slocum yelled. "And the killing of ole Ziggie. Well, what do you say?"

"Bullshit," said the voice.

"Listen," Slocum called out. "I don't want to see anyone killed out here this morning. Come on down."

A rifle shot rang out, and dust was kicked up just a few feet from where Slocum sat. The Appaloosa jumped. Slocum turned him and raced back to where the rest of his posse waited.

"Well, what now?" said Rance.

"I guess it's a fight," Slocum said. "But there's something funny here."

"What?"

"I ain't sure. It's awful quiet."

"Well, what do we do?"

"We got no cover out here," Slocum said. "Rance, you take three men and move way over yonder to the right. Stay out of range. When you get way over there, move on in close to the mountain, and then start working your way close to the mine office. I'll take the other three and go to the left and do the same thing."

"All right," Rance said. He pointed to three men and started to ride, the three following along.

"Okay, boys," said Slocum to the remaining three. "Let's go."

They moved in from the two sides, and then Slocum fired the first shot at the mine office. Suddenly shots were fired from all eight men. There was no fire returned from the office. Slocum hollered out for the posse to cease firing. It took a while, but they did at last stop shooting, and Slocum called out again.

"Hey, you up there. You ready to give it up?"

A face appeared in the window, and a rifle barrel came out, firing another shot. Slocum fired back, and a second barrage of bullets came from the posse. The face disappeared. Soon the posse stopped firing again. An arm appeared in the window, the rifle in its hand. It tossed the rifle out, and as it clattered down the side of the mountain, the voice from inside called out, "All right. All right. You win. Don't shoot no more."

"Come on out the front door with your hands high," Slocum yelled.

"All right. All right. Don't shoot."

In another minute, the door to the mine office opened, and a figure stepped out onto the landing. Its hands were up. Slocum prepared to move in, but just then a shot rang out, and the figure crumpled, collapsed and tumbled down the long stairway.

"Don't shoot, damn it," Slocum cried out, as he ran toward the fallen man. Dropping down beside him, Slocum quickly discovered that the shot had been a true one. The man was dead. "Damn it."

The rest of the posse had come up by then to stand around Slocum and look at the dead man.

"Damn it," Slocum said. "Who the hell fired that shot?"

"I did it, Slocum," said Rance. "He had another gun."

"I never saw it," Slocum said. "Anyone else see it?"

No one answered.

"Well, where the hell is it?"

"He must have dropped it up there when I hit him," Rance said.

"Is there anyone else here?" said one of the cowhands, looking around nervously.

"That's what's been bothering me," said Slocum. "You men go over to the mine entrance and check it out. Be careful. Rance, come on with me."

Slocum led the way up the stairs, his Colt ready for any surprise. All the way, he was looking for any sign of a gun that the dead man might have dropped. He saw none. He stood for a moment on the landing looking at the open doorway. Then he moved into the office. No one was there. He stepped back out onto the landing where Rance waited and looked over toward the mine entrance. One of the cowhands saw him and called out, "There's no one here."

Slocum went back into the office and looked around. He noticed that the door to the safe was standing open. He found no money, no books. The place was abandoned. Just the old Sharps buffalo gun stood in the corner gathering dust.

"Damn," he said. "They've cleared out. They're gone."

Slocum went outside and back down the stairs. Some of the cowhands were already studying the ground. "Over here, Mr. Slocum," said one of the boys. Slocum walked over to where the young man was pointing at the ground. "Several horses rode out of here not long ago," the boy said. "And the last thing that went out was a wagon. 'Pears to have been loaded heavy too."

"Why would they have cleared out just before we came up here?" Slocum said, not really asking anyone for an answer.

The cowboy shrugged. "Maybe they just figgered it was time to get," he said.

"They left that one fellow to hold us up some," Slocum said. "I'd say that means they didn't leave too long before we got here. I'd also say they're trying to get out with one more wagon load of ore. That'll go on up to Complacency if I don't miss my guess."

"Complacency?" said Rance.

"It's over in the next territory," Slocum explained. "It's where they been selling the ore. I don't think we all need to go over there. Soon as we cross that line, we'll just be ordinary citizens again. I'll take four of these boys with me, Rance. You take the other two and ride back to the ranch. Tell them what we found out here, and tell Marla that we're on the trail of Charlie Dode and the rest."

"I think I oughta go with you, Slocum."

"You're foreman of the ranch. I don't know how long this'll take. You need to be back running things."

"Well—"

"Go on now. Don't argue with me."

"All right. Who's going back with me?"

"You two," Slocum said, pointing at two of the men. "You all go on now. We'll bury this poor fellow."

Rance and the two cowhands started back toward the

ranch. Slocum turned toward one of the remaining four. "Did you see a shovel up there anywhere?"

"Yeah. I think so."

"Go get it."

As the young man went for the shovel, Slocum stood watching the other three as they disappeared down the road. Yeah, there was something funny going on all right. And he meant to get to the bottom of it.

13

That man had a mother and a father, Slocum thought, maybe brothers and sisters, as he watched the cowhands unceremoniously dump the body into the shallow grave they had dug. If any of them are still alive, they'll never know what became of him. They'll always wonder. That Dode didn't give a shit. Slocum wondered what Dode had said to the man to get him to stay behind and try to hold off the posse that way. He had to have promised him something, or told him there was really no danger. Some damn lie.

Then again, there wasn't really any serious danger. The man had done his job. He'd held up the posse for a time and then surrendered to go to jail and be charged with—what? He'd be safely on his way to jail right now had not ole Rance thought that he'd seen a gun. Once in jail, he'd have to stand trial, and maybe Dode had promised him a hell of a good lawyer. With all the money he'd stole from the mine, he could sure afford that.

Well, it was a shitty world, and the best a man could do was go through it minding his own business. But minding one's own business was not always easy, as Slocum could damn well swear to. He thought about how this business had all started for him. He had been lying on his cot in the bunkhouse with no worries other than that damn gray horse. And look at him now. Tracking murderers and thieves for someone else, someone he had not even known a short while ago. Musing in this manner, he watched as the cowhands tossed the last shovelful of dirt onto the fresh grave. Then he looked at the road toward the ranch. Rance and the other boys had disappeared from sight.

"Come on, boys," he said. "We got some tracking to do."

They followed the tracks, which were clear. Dode, the escaping miners and the wagon were all riding the same trail. It became obvious the farther they rode, however, that the wagon had fallen behind. The horseback riders were moving at a faster clip than was the heavily loaded wagon. Slocum thought more about Dode and tried to figure his thinking. Now, if I was escaping with a load of silver ore, he told himself, and I had me a bunch of men, wouldn't I want to stay close to the stuff to protect it? Dode was apparently more concerned with protecting his own hide. Whoever was driving the wagon, and riding in it, Dode was willing to sacrifice, just as he had sacrificed the man back at the mine.

There was no way of knowing how many men were in the wagon though. There could be anywhere from one to four. Six maybe? It would depend partly on how much ore was loaded. It wasn't long before Slocum knew where they were headed. They were on the road to Complacency all right. Dode intended to sell the ore at the same place as before, then probably split the money with his men and scatter. It seemed stupid, in a way. Maybe he thought that the man he left behind would kill Slocum. Or at least, he thought that the poor fool would be able to hold them back longer. Whatever it was, Slocum had a feeling that this was all too easy. He thought again about the fact that Dode had abandoned the mine unexpectedly, almost as if he had known that the posse was coming. But why go back to Complacency?

Marla and Rance were in the bedroom with Doc, Hettie, and Burl Johnson. They were quiet as long as Doc was busy examining Johnson, but as soon as Doc straightened up, they all seemed to start in at once.

"Hold your horses," Doc said. "I can't hear myself think. Now, Burl's doing just fine. I'd say maybe tomorrow, you can try to get him up out of bed. Let him walk around a little. Start getting his strength back. Take it easy though. Don't overdo it. Just a little each day for a week or so. I'll be checking in regular to make sure things are going right. Another couple of weeks, maybe, he can even go back to town. Maybe."

"That's great, Doc," said Rance.

"But don't worry about him staying here just as long as he needs to," said Marla. "He's hardly any trouble at all, especially with Hettie here."

"Well, that's just fine," Doc said. "I'll be running along now. Hettie, have you got everything you need? Not running low on anything, are you?"

"I'm just fine, Doc," said Hettie.

"Well, be seeing you then."

"Doc," said Johnson, "thanks again."

"Don't think nothing of it," said Doc. "It's my job. And you're the protector of this community. We got to keep you around."

The doc left the room, and Marla followed him to the door. Soon she was back in the room with the others.

"Now, Rance," said Johnson, "you can finish telling us what happened out there this morning."

"Like I was saying," said Rance, "Slocum rode up ahead of us and called out to the mine. He told them he was a deputy and they was under arrest. He was answered by a rifle shot, so he come hightailing it back where we was waiting for him, and then he split us up, and we attacked them from two sides. Well, by and by, a fellow throws a rifle out the window and hollers out that he's had enough. Slocum tells him to come on out, but he come out on the landing there with a revolver in his hand, and I shot him. He was the only one there."

"Charlie Dode?" said Marla.

"Gone. A heavy loaded wagon was gone. Everybody was gone. All except that one man. The safe was open and empty.

The books was gone. Everything. Slocum told me to bring two boys with me and come on back here and tell you what happened, and him and the other four, I guess, are on Charlie and them's trail."

"I wonder how come Charlie decided to get out last night," Marla said. "He didn't know that we had any real evidence, did he?"

"Did he know that Slocum had followed that other wagon over to Complacency?" Rance asked.

"I'd say he was warned," said Johnson.

"Warned?" said Rance. "Well, who could've warned him? Who would have?"

"That part ain't so easy, Rance," said Johnson, "but there's a lot of money involved. You know, you had ole Tobe working on the ranch as a cowhand, and he was involved with Dode."

"Yeah, that's right," Rance said. "I guess there could be others."

"It would only take one to carry a warning," said Johnson.

"If I find out who it is," said Marla, "I'll kill the son of a bitch."

"No you won't, Marla," said Johnson. "If you find out who it is, you tell me. All right?"

"Oh, all right."

The four young cowhands riding with Slocum, Tex, Bandy, Curly, and Harry, were anxious to catch up with their prey, but Slocum held them back. He made them ride easy. "We know where they're going," he told them. "We just don't know how they're split up. It also looks to me like they knew we were coming to the mine. If I'm right about that, they'll know that we're on the trail, so they'll be ready for us. At least, they think they will. Just be patient, boys. We'll get them."

The sun was low in the western sky when Slocum decided that the wagon would have to stop for the night. He still could not see it anywhere ahead, but the tracks were still clear. He rode a little longer, looking for a likely spot, and then he stopped. "Make us a little camp here, boys," he said. "I'm going to scout ahead a ways."

He rode on, leaving the cowhands to prepare a camp for the night, but after a short ride, he swung wide off the trail. In a while, he spotted it. The wagon was stopped beside the road. A small fire was burning. The thieves were not too worried. He moved in closer for a better look. It looked like four men were lounging around the wagon. He turned the Appaloosa and rode back to his own camp.

"They've stopped up there for the night, boys," he said. "Four of them with the wagon. The rest have gone on ahead. Get a good night's rest, and we'll hit them in the morning."

"Mr. Slocum," asked Bandy, "how're we going to do it?"

"We'll have to see what it looks like in the morning," Slocum said, "but right now, I'm thinking that we'll just ride right up to them. I'll tell them they're under arrest. If they give up quiet, that'll be fine. If they start shooting, so will we."

It didn't take long for Slocum and the cowhands to catch up with the wagon the following morning. "Get ready," Slocum said, and each man got a gun in his hand. They rode slowly toward the wagon. The man in the rear of the wagon turned his head to see them coming and shouted a warning to his companions. The wagon stopped, and all four men jumped out and on the other side, readying their weapons. Slocum stopped his small posse.

"You up there," he called out. "We're duly deputized lawmen, and we're carrying warrants for your arrest. Give it up peaceful and ride back to Rascality with us, and no one'll get hurt."

"How do we know you're lawmen?"

"If you'll put down your guns and come out from behind that box, I'll show you the papers signed by Sheriff Johnson," Slocum said.

"Burl Johnson's dead."

"That's what you think," said Slocum. "And you wouldn't be thinking that either if ole Tobe hadn't told you he shot Burl."

Slocum's answer was a rifle shot that knocked Bandy backward off his horse. Slocum and the other three cowhands dismounted and started shooting back. One of the miners behind the wagon jerked, a splotch of red on his forehead. Then he crumpled and disappeared from sight. Slocum got one in the right shoulder, but the man screamed and pulled a six-gun with his left hand. A moment later, he dropped, a bullet in his chest. Tex and Curly ran wide around the wagon and shot from the sides, killing the last two. Suddenly it was deathly quiet. In the silence, a wagon horse farted.

Slocum knelt beside Bandy, as the others ran over to see how badly their partner was hurt. Slocum looked up at them. "Sorry, boys," he said. "He's gone. Load him into the wagon. We'll take him back to the ranch." Then he stood and walked over to the wagon. He first checked to make sure that the four miners were indeed dead. Then he looked in the wagon bed. It was loaded with silver ore. Two of the cowhands laid Bandy's body out on top of the load.

"Tex," said Slocum, "you and Curly take this wagon back to the ranch. Tell Miss Marla what happened out here, and tell her that me and Harry are going on to Complacency."

"Yes, sir," said Tex. Then he looked down at the bodies of the outlaws. "What about them?" he asked.

"They'll feed the coyotes and the buzzards," said Slocum. "Let's get going."

As Slocum and Harry mounted up, Tex and Curly tied their horses onto the back of the wagon. Then they climbed up onto the seat, Curly took up the reins, and they started back toward the ranch. Slocum waved, then started riding toward Complacency, Harry riding along beside him.

"How many men we going to be facing in Complacency, Mr. Slocum?" Harry asked.

"They told me that Dode had a dozen men working at the mine," Slocum said. "We've killed five."

"That leaves seven," Harry said.

"Eight counting Dode," said Slocum.

"Eight men and two of us. How come you sent two men back to the ranch with the wagon?"

"There's still someone back there," Slocum told him. "Whoever it was that warned Dode we was coming."

They rode on for a while in silence, and then Slocum said, "You scared, Harry?"

"Well, yeah, I reckon I am, a little."

"You want to ride back to the ranch?"

"I'm riding with you, Mr. Slocum."

"Well, if you mean to hang with me," Slocum said, "stop calling me mister."

"Yes, sir," Harry said. "Uh, what do I call you?"

"Slocum will do just fine."

"Yes, sir, Slocum."

They made it into Complacency after dark that night, but the town was still alive. Slocum headed toward the sheriff's office. "We need to check in here," he told Harry. They stopped and tied their horses at the hitch rail. "You can come in with me or wait here," Slocum said.

"I'll wait," said Harry. Slocum went on inside and found the sheriff sitting behind his desk. The lawman seemed surprised to see Slocum.

"Howdy," said Slocum.

"Slocum, is it?" the sheriff said.

"You know it is, and I believe I heard you called Mac."

"Mac Sowles," the sheriff said, reaching out a hand, which Slocum shook.

"Well, Mac, I'm kind of in your game now, but I hope it's real temporary."

Mac wrinkled his face in puzzlement as Slocum pulled out the paper with which Burl Johnson had deputized him. Slocum handed the paper to Mac. "I'm out of my jurisdiction. I know that. That's why I came to see you first."

"First?"

"Well, I didn't want to just go to killing folks without checking in."

"What're you talking about, Slocum?"

"You recall I told you that Charlie Dode was robbing ole man Ziggie's mine?"

"I recall that."

"Well, Burl Johnson deputized me and a handful of cowhands to deal with it. We rode out to the mine, and Dode and his whole crew had cleared out. We followed them here. Charlie Dode is wanted for the killing of Ziggie as well as for stealing all that money."

"Well, you ain't legal in this territory, Slocum."

"That's why I came here."

"What do you want me to do?"

"I want you to either help me out or stay out of my way," Slocum said. "It's up to you."

"I don't like it, Slocum. If you go to killing Dode and them over here, I'm afraid I'll have to arrest you. You see, they ain't wanted over here."

"You mean if they cross the line after they murder someone, it's okay?"

"Well, there's legalities to consider."

"I reckon there are," Slocum said, "but I ain't letting Dode and them get away with what they done."

"Look, Slocum. It's late now. Likely we couldn't find them if we went looking for them. Why don't you check yourself into a room and get a good night's rest. Come back over here in the morning, and we'll figure this thing out. All right?"

Slocum looked at the sheriff of Complacency for a moment. Then he said, "All right, Mac. I'll be here in the morning. Early."

"Yeah. See you then."

Slocum stepped out onto the sidewalk and closed the door behind him. He said in a low voice, "Harry, take your horse and go for a walk down the street. But keep your eye on this door."

Harry loosened the reins from the hitch rail and started walking. Slocum stood there another moment, then mounted his Appaloosa and rode toward the livery stable, thinking about what a suspicious son of a bitch he had become lately. Goddamn all these people anyhow, he thought. Goddamn them all to hell.

14

He got the big Appaloosa settled in well for the night and then walked back the way he had come. He soon met Harry on the sidewalk. "I don't know what you was wanting me to watch for, Slocum," the cowhand said, "but soon as you got on down the road a ways, that sheriff come out of his office."

"Where'd he go?" Slocum asked.

"He went to the hotel, but he went around to the back side to go in. I don't know where he went after that."

"I got me an idea," Slocum said. "Why don't you take your horse on down to the livery. I'll go in here and get us a room for the night." He jerked a thumb toward the hotel just by them.

"Okay," said Harry, swinging into the saddle. "I'll meet you back here."

"In the saloon," Slocum said. As Harry rode toward the stable, Slocum went into the hotel. He paid for a room and took the key. Then he walked into the adjacent saloon and ordered a bottle of whiskey and two glasses. He casually looked over the crowd as he found himself a vacant table. He sat down and poured himself a drink. In another couple of minutes, Harry walked in, and Slocum waved him over. He poured Harry a drink. "Thanks, Slocum," Harry said, taking it up for a sip.

Slocum leaned forward and spoke low. "You recognize anyone in here?"

Harry lifted his glass for another sip and looked around, trying to appear casual. "Can't say I do," he said.

"Well, I don't either, but I'll tell you what I'm thinking. I'm thinking that Dode and them are here in town somewhere, likely in this very hotel. I think that's what that damn sheriff was up to. I think he was warning Dode about us being here. I'm a bit slow thinking sometimes, but I think that Dode has got the lawman here on his payroll. That would explain how come him to throw me in the can last time I was here. To give that wagon time to get clear of me. He was awful hesitant a while ago about cooperating with me too. Told me to come back in the morning."

"So what the hell are we going to do?" Harry asked.

"I'll go see him in the morning," Slocum said. "What he tells me then will cinch it up one way or the other. Why don't you go on up to the room. It's number six up the stairs. I'll come up later." Slocum laid the key on the table, and he noticed Harry looking at the bottle. "Take that with you," he added. As Harry took the bottle and headed for the room, Slocum thought about Dode. He would sure be surprised when his wagon failed to show up. They should be looking for it in the morning. He tried to consider what he was going to do, but he couldn't really come up with anything. It was like he had told Harry. Everything depended on the answer he would get from Sheriff Mac Sowles in the morning. If Sowles turned out to be legitimate and agreed to help, then everything should work out all right. But if Slocum's suspicions turned out to be true, he and Harry could wind up having to fight their way out of town.

He considered this ring of culprits he had uncovered. Charlie Dode had placed ole Tobe on the ranch as a cowhand. Either that or he had somehow recruited the bastard to work for him. Now it sure looked like he had the sheriff of Complacency on his payroll too. And there was still someone back at the ranch, the one who had warned Dode that it was time to clear out. This was quite a network of thieves that

Dode had working with him, and they had been stealing silver ore from the mine and rustling cattle from the ranch. Slocum wondered how far this whole business would lead before he had rooted them all out.

Tex and Curly were still moving along the road in the wagon. They had made it back to the ranch, but they were still a good distance from the ranch house. They had discussed stopping for the night, but had decided to keep going.

"Slocum told us to get on back and tell Miss Marla what the hell was up," said Curly. "The road ain't bad. If we keep moving slow like this, we oughta be all right."

"Yeah. I reckon you're right," Tex said.

They kept moving, and in a few minutes, Tex said, "Hey. Someone's riding toward us." He pulled out his revolver and held it ready. Curly hauled back on the reins to stop the wagon. He was about to pick up his revolver when Tex stopped him. "It's all right," he said. "It's ole Rance." He put his revolver away.

Rance rode up closer. "Curly? Tex? That you?"

"Yeah," said Tex. "Man, are we glad to see you. I'll sure feel better three of us escorting this stuff to the ranch than just the two of us here."

"What have you got there?" Rance asked.

"After we rode on out," Curly said, "we caught up with this wagon. There was four men with it, and Slocum tried to put them under arrest, but they went to shooting, so we killed them all. Then Slocum told us to bring this back to the ranch and tell y'all what happened."

"A load of ore?" said Rance, riding up close for a better look. Then he saw the body. "Who's that you're hauling with it?"

"That's poor ole Bandy," Curly said. "He took the first shot in the fracas. Slocum told us to just leave them others out there for the buzzards."

"And the coyotes," Tex added.

"Yeah," Rance said. "That's good enough for them. Where were you boys headed with this wagon?"

"Back to the ranch house," Tex said.

"Well, there's been a change of plans," said Rance. "Follow me."

Rance turned his horse and headed north across the open range. Tex gave Curly a curious look, and Curly shrugged and whipped up the horses to follow Rance. It was a rougher ride across the prairie than on the road, so they moved even slower than before. Once, they almost got the wagon stuck in a rut, but they managed to get it going again. It was almost daylight before Rance led them into a small, nearly hidden canyon on the far reaches of the Circle Z. As they rolled into the canyon, Tex and Curly could hear the sounds of cattle.

"Right there's good enough," Rance said. "Let's get those horses unhitched."

The two cowhands got out of the wagon and went to work. They got the horses loose, and Curly looked up at Rance, who was still in his saddle. "What do we do with them?" he asked.

"Just turn them loose," said Rance. "Now, you boys climb on your own horses, and let's ride on back to the ranch house. You can report to Marla and to Burl Johnson everything that happened out here."

"All right," said Curly, walking to the rear of the wagon to get his horse. Tex followed. They untied the reins of their horses and swung up into their saddles just in time for Rance's two bullets to tear into their backs knocking them out of the saddle again. Tex was dead when he hit the ground. Curly landed on his back. His right hand reached for his revolver, and through teeth clenched in agony, he said, "Rance, you—"

Rance sent a second slug into his chest to kill him.

Slocum was at the sheriff's office in Complacency early in the morning. The night before, he had gone to the stable and located the horses of Dode and the miners, and he had cut all their cinch straps. He was anxious to see Mac Sowles and find out what the sheriff had to say, but the door was still locked. He had told Harry to hang out at the hotel, but to keep his eyes open and watch the street. If anything happened to Slocum, Harry was to ride back to the ranch and report it to Marla and Burl Johnson. He wasn't sure, but he didn't think that anyone in Complacency knew Harry. They had been seen together for only a few minutes, and, as far as Slocum could tell, not by anyone who knew them. He took a cigar out of his pocket, struck a match and lit it. Then he saw the sheriff coming.

"Morning, Sheriff," he said as Sowles approached the office door, key in hand.

"Morning," said Sowles, opening the door. He walked on in, and Slocum followed him. Sowles sat down behind his desk, and Slocum dragged up a chair and sat opposite him. He puffed on his cigar waiting for the sheriff to say something. At last, tired of waiting, he said, "Well?"

Sowles looked up at him, not responding.

"So what the hell did you decide?" Slocum asked him. "Are you with me on this thing?"

"I can't be, Slocum," said Sowles. "I checked. Dode and them ain't done nothing in this territory. There ain't a thing I can do about it without papers. You got to go back to Rascality and get the proper papers all filled out and signed, and then you got to bring them papers back here and present them to the judge. Then he can tell me to go on and give you a hand. Without all that, there ain't a thing I can do."

"I know those men are in town," Slocum said, "and if I go all the way back to Rascality for papers, they'll be long gone before I can get back here. Damn it, Sowles, I got to get them while I have a chance."

"You make a move on them, Slocum," said Sowles, "and I'll have to arrest you for it."

"Where are they?" said Slocum.

"What makes you think—"

"That's where you went after I left here last night, ain't it?" Slocum said. "To warn Dode? You left here and went to the hotel, and you went in through the back door."

"How the hell do you—"

Slocum pulled out his Colt and cocked it, leveling it at Sowles. "Stand up slow," he said.

"Slocum, you're making a big mistake here."

"Shut up and shuck that gun belt."

Sowles unfastened the buckle and laid the gun belt on his desk.

"Now get over there in that cell," Slocum said.

"Now look here—"

"Move it."

Sowles moved into the cell, and Slocum shut the door and locked it.

"Now you can take off your clothes," he said.

"What?"

"You heard me. Strip."

"What for?"

"I figure a naked sheriff in his own cell won't holler for help," Slocum said. "When I leave here, I'll lock your front door so no one'll come walking in on you. When I'm done with Dode and his gang, I'll come back here and give you your britches and your keys. No one'll be the wiser. Now get out of them clothes."

"Slocum, I swear to God, I'll kill you for this."

"If you don't hurry it up, I'll kill you right now. This Colt's got a hair trigger."

Slocum leveled the Colt at Sowles, and Sowles started unfastening his britches.

Back out on the street, Slocum saw some men hanging around the Assay Office. He didn't recognize them, but he guessed that they were some of Dode's miners waiting for their stolen wagon load of ore. They'd have a long wait, he thought. He did not see Charlie Dode anywhere. Likely, Sowles had warned Dode, and Dode was keeping his distance. Slocum walked down the street toward the hotel, and he found Harry standing on the sidewalk.

"You see them men down yonder?" Harry asked.

"I see them," said Slocum. "I suspect they're some of Dode's gang."

"That's what I figured," Harry said. "I ain't seen no sign of Dode though."

"He's likely in some hole waiting to see how things develop," Slocum said. "Listen. I got me an idea. I'm going to find out if there's a judge or even a mayor in this damn town. I'd like to talk to someone with some authority before we just go shooting the place up."

"What about the sheriff?" Harry asked.

"I think he's in on it," said Slocum. "I locked him up naked in his own cell."

Harry laughed, and then he said, "I reckon that ought to keep him quiet for a while anyhow."

"Yeah. That's what I thought."

"What do you want me to do while you're hunting the judge or whoever?"

"Just what you've been doing," Slocum told him. "Keep your eye on that bunch down there."

"Okay."

It didn't take Slocum long to find out that there was no judge in Complacency, but the town did have a mayor. Slocum found the mayor in his office sitting behind a big desk. He walked up to the desk and said, "I'm John Slocum."

The little man behind the desk looked up, extended his hand, and said, "I'm Boyd Hager, mayor of this burg. What can I do for you?"

Slocum took out the paper signed by Sheriff Johnson to prove that he was an authorized deputy sheriff, and he told the mayor the whole story of the theft at the Circle Z. "I've tracked them here, Mayor," he said, "but I can't get no cooperation out of your sheriff. I hope he ain't your brother-in-law or nothing like that, because I suspect him of taking some payoff from Charlie Dode." He went on to detail the ways in which the sheriff had seemed to be blocking his path. "Now, I got the bunch of miners right here in town, and I'd like to try to arrest them and take them back to Rascality, but Sowles, he says that if I try anything like that, he'll have to arrest me."

"I've known ole Ziggie for years," said Hager. "I was real

sorry to hear about his death. And you say Burl Johnson is laid up at his house?"

"That's right," said Slocum.

"And Mac won't help you?"

"No sir. He won't."

Hager leaned back in his chair with a heavy sigh. He scratched his head. Then he stood up.

"Slocum," he said, "this is a tough one. I believe you. I've been a little bit suspicious of Mac Sowles for some time now, but I didn't have anything on him. It's tough to act on just what you tell me though. You can understand that."

"Yes, sir, but—"

"Hold on. I ain't through. I've got an idea. You come along with me."

Hager led the way out of the office and down the street, Slocum following along. A few doors down, Hager turned into the bank. He said hello to some customers and tellers as he walked straight back to the president's office. "Julian," he said, "I got to ask a favor of you, and it's a little bit irregular. Oh, this here is Mr. Slocum from over across the line. He's a deputy sheriff."

Julian nodded at Slocum, and Slocum said, "Howdy."

"Well, Mr. Mayor," said Julian, "what is it you want?"

"I want you to show me the records of Mac Sowles's bank account."

"Well, that's—"

"Irregular," said Hager. "I know. I've already said it. You know I wouldn't ask you to do anything irregular if there wasn't good reason for it."

"Well, yes."

"Well then?"

"I'll, uh, I'll just fetch them." He got up and left the room.

Hager looked at Slocum. "This won't take long," he said. In another couple of minutes, Julian walked back into the office with some papers. He started to walk back around his desk with them, but the mayor took them out of his hand and studied them for a bit. He tossed the papers onto the banker's desk. "Thanks, Julian," he said. "Let's go, Slocum."

Slocum followed the mayor back out of the bank and back to his office. Once in the office, Hager said, "Slocum, it's not yet proof, but it's close. There's way too much money in that account for Mac to have on his salary. Now, here's what I'm going to do. I'm going to appoint you deputy long enough for you to do what you have to do with this Charlie Dode and his crew. I want this business all cleared up as soon as possible. By the way, where is Mac Sowles?"

"I locked him naked in his jail cell," Slocum said.

15

Slocum strolled back to where Harry still waited patiently, watching the miners hanging around on the sidewalk. He sidled up to Harry. "What's up?" Harry asked.

"Have you seen any sign of ole Dode?" Slocum asked.

"Nary," said Harry.

"Well, I got us all legal here," Slocum said. "We're going to have to do something. I went down to the stable and cut all these boys cinches, but if anything starts up here, some of them might just jump on any handy horse and try to make an escape. I think I'll just go down to the stable and saddle up our horses and bring them down here before we stir up anything."

"I'm just standing here waiting," said Harry.

"Not for much longer," Slocum said. He turned and walked to the stable and saddled up Harry's horse and his own big Appaloosa. Then he mounted the Appaloosa and led the other and rode back toward where Harry waited, but along the way, he stopped by the sheriff's office. Dismounting, he tied both horses to the hitch rail there and walked into the office.

"Goddamn you, Slocum," Sowles hollered. "Give me my britches and let me out of here."

"Be patient, Mac," Slocum said, walking over to the gun

rack. He selected a pair of Greeners, loaded them up, and headed for the door.

"Slocum," Sowles yelled. "What the hell are you up to? You get back here. Goddamn you, I'll kill you, you son of a bitch."

Slocum walked the two horses back to where Harry waited, dismounted, and tied them to a hitch rail. Then he moved back to Harry's side and handed one of the shotguns to the young cowboy.

"You ready?" he asked.

"As I'll ever be," Harry said.

Slocum eyed the group of miners. There were six of them, a hard-looking bunch. The shotguns would come in handy. So far, they did not seem to be suspecting anything. "Let's go," Slocum said, and he and Harry headed for the gang. They had gotten fairly close before one of the miners noticed them coming. The man slapped one of his companions on the shoulder and pointed. Slocum and Harry stopped.

"You men are under arrest," Slocum said. "Before any of you say anything, let me tell you that I'm deputized on both sides of the line now. I want you to all drop your guns on the sidewalk."

"What do you say, Pete?" one of the men asked.

The man called Pete answered, "There's only two of them."

"But them two scatterguns they got could take out all of us."

"We better do what he says. Hell, they got no proof of anything anyhow."

The men all unbuckled their side arms and dropped them, and Slocum and Harry marched them back to the jail. There were two cells, and Slocum put the bunch of miners in the cell next door to the naked sheriff.

"Damn you, Slocum," Sowles said. He was sitting on the cot with the blanket over his lap. "You give me back my britches."

"Shut up," said Slocum. "Come on, Harry."

They left the jail and went back to the mayor's office.

Boyd Hager was still in. He looked up at Slocum with curiosity.

"I've locked all them miners in the jail," Slocum said. "But Dode and two others are missing. I need to go look for them. I don't know if we got anything on that bunch over here, but you reckon it's all right for me to hold them there for a spell?"

"You can hold them there as long as you need to, Slocum," Hager said. "I mean to have me a talk with Judge Dotson soon as he gets to town. I wired him already this morning after our talk. He's coming. We'll figure out how to best deal with all this. In the meantime, they're all right just where you got them."

"Thanks, Mr. Mayor. Harry, let's go find Dode and them other two."

Slocum and Harry went to the hotel where they found out that Charlie Dode had already paid the bill and left. They went to the stable and discovered that Dode's and two other horses were gone. "Damn," Slocum said, "where would the son of a bitch go? He left them others hanging around here waiting for that wagon. He must have been afraid that something would happen here, or else he'd still be here."

"Yeah," Harry said. "There would have been a good pay-off."

They searched all around the stable, but it was impossible to find any tracks that could be followed. "They could have left out of here in any damn direction, Slocum," Harry said. They headed back for the jail where they questioned all the prisoners, but no one would admit to knowing anything. Slocum overheard the man called Pete grumble to one of the others, "The son of a bitch run out on us, didn't he?" At last, Slocum gave it up. He talked with Hager once more before leaving Complacency, and along the way back to the Circle Z, he and Harry looked for any sign they might come across, but they didn't find any.

Back at the ranch, though, they did find Burl Johnson sitting up in the living room. Harry went back to work with the other cowhands, and Slocum sat in the big house visiting with Johnson and Marla. Rance, Marla said, was out taking care of ranch business. Slocum told them how he and Harry had captured the batch of miners in Complacency, how the sheriff was in on the whole mess, how they had been deputized over there, and how the mayor was going to talk with the judge about how to deal with them.

"I'm just as glad I didn't have to bring them all back here to Rascality with me," he said.

"They can likely try them over there," Johnson said. "They were selling stolen ore there, and if Sowles was taking bribes from them, well, that's just more reason."

"I'm just sorry that I didn't get Dode," Slocum said. "At least we saved the wagon load of silver. Where'd you have it put, Marla?"

"What are you talking about?" Marla asked.

Slocum leaned forward in his chair. "They were trying to steal one last wagon load," he said. "We stopped them, and I sent it back here with Tex and Curly."

"I haven't seen any wagon," Marla said, "and I haven't seen Tex and Curly either."

"Shit," Slocum said. He jumped up, got his hat, and headed for the door.

"Slocum," said Marla. "Where the hell're you going?"

"I'll be back," he said. He hurried to the corral and saddled his Appaloosa again, and he started to retrace the road to Complacency. He rode most of the rest of that day, and he had to stop and make a camp for the night. He went to sleep asking himself what could have gone wrong. What could have happened to the wagon and the two cowboys? Charlie Dode and the others had been ahead of them on the trail. He had thought everything was well under control.

Then it came to him, and he cursed himself for not having thought of it before. He should have realized it when they had arrived at the mine to find it abandoned, well, almost abandoned. The person, or persons, back at the ranch or in Rascality who had warned Dode that they were coming. He had to be the one. Slocum did not sleep well that night.

• • •

Johnson was back in bed, and Hettie was sitting with him in the room when Marla heard a knock at her door. She went to answer it and found Rance there. He walked in and took her in his arms, but she pushed him away. "What's wrong, Marla?" he asked.

"Where have you been the last few nights?" she asked.

"I've had work to do," he said. "What with the rustlers and that business out at the mine. Besides all that, this is a big ranch to run. I'd have come to you if I could. You ought to know that."

"I waited for you. You didn't even send me any word. Where were you, Rance?"

"I told you. I had things to do. Last night I was riding the range watching over the cattle. I had reason to believe that the rustlers might strike again last night, and I wanted to make sure that everything was covered. I've had the boys all stretched way too thin lately." He reached for Marla again and pulled her in close to him. "I missed you," he said. "Don't you think I'd rather have been here with you than out riding the range? I'd have been here if I could. You know that."

He kissed her again, and this time she did not resist. "Oh, Rance," she said, "it's just that—"

"I know. I know," he said. "These times are hard on everyone. But try to be patient. It'll all be over with real soon."

"God, I hope so," she said. "I want to see that Charlie Dode dead. Do you really think that he's still got rustlers out there? Slocum said that he abandoned the mine and ran away."

"We don't know where he ran to though," Rance said. "He could have a hideout somewhere around these parts and still be operating."

"Damn him."

"We'll get him, Marla. Don't worry. For right now, just try to put him out of your mind. Come on over here and sit down. Come on."

He led her over to the couch and sat beside her, putting

his arm around her shoulders, and she leaned into him.

"Marla," he said.

"What?"

"There's something I want to ask you."

"Well, what is it?"

"Something very important."

"Well, go on."

"Marla, will you marry me?"

"What?"

"You heard me right, Marla. I want to marry you."

"Oh, Rance," she said, "just because we—"

"That's a part of it, of course," Rance said. "You're wonderful. And I love you. I really do. Besides all that, it makes good sense, now doesn't it? You own the ranch now, and I've been running the ranch all along. I did the job for Ziggie, and now I'm doing it for you. What could be a better match?"

"It does kind of make sense, when you put it like that, Rance," Marla said, "but, well, I haven't even been thinking like that. I've had so much on my mind."

"Well, think about it, darlin'," Rance said. "Think about it real hard. Okay? I don't want to wait forever for your answer. You think you could give me an answer tomorrow?"

"I don't know, Rance."

"All right. I won't say anything more about it till then. Come on. Come with me."

Rance stood up and pulled Marla to her feet. Then he led her toward her bedroom. They went inside and shut the door behind them.

Slocum woke up the following morning and saddled his horse. He didn't bother with a fire or breakfast or coffee. He started riding and watching the trail carefully. Soon he was almost back to the spot where he had left Tex and Curly with the wagon, and he spotted the place where the wagon had left the road.

"Damn," he said out loud. "How did I miss this before?"

The answer, of course, was that he hadn't been watching

for it. He had not anticipated any trouble with the wagon and the two cowhands. The tracks were not the plainest he had ever followed, and his going was slow. He could sometimes make out the prints of the two horses that were tied on behind, and once or twice, he thought that he could make out where a third horse was riding along beside them, but he wasn't sure. If there had been a third horse, who could have been on it, and what could he have been up to? It had to be someone the cowboys knew and trusted to just ride along with them like that. And where the hell were they going? He had an idea about the person, but he did not want to say it. Not even to himself. He could be wrong. He had other reasons, personal reasons, for disliking the man, and he did not want those personal reasons to cause him to accuse the man of these things.

He kept riding, hoping that there would be some good explanation for all of this, but he couldn't imagine what it could be. It was early afternoon when he saw the entrance to the small canyon ahead. He rode into it slowly. The first thing he saw was the wagon. It no longer had the horses hitched to it. Looking around carefully, he rode ahead. He saw that the wagon was still loaded. Someone had put it here for some reason. To come back for it later? Then he saw the bodies of the two cowboys.

"Oh, God," he said. He rode on over and dismounted. Kneeling beside them, he rolled them onto their backs and folded their arms over their chests. He took note of the fact that they had both been shot in the back, and neither man had begun to pull his revolver. Whatever happened out here, he told himself, they had not been expecting it. There had been a third rider, and it had been someone they knew and trusted. The third rider must have told them to drive to this canyon, and not just anyone could have made them do that. It all became clear. Damn, he felt stupid.

Rance. It had to be Rance. And it had been Rance all along. Rance had been working with Dode, stealing silver and rustling cattle. Rance. The son of a bitch. That's the reason he killed the man back at the mine. The man had not had a gun at all. Rance had killed the poor son of a bitch to keep him quiet. It had been Rance who warned Dode to clear out. And Rance had met these two poor boys on the road and told them to drive to this canyon. They had done it because he was the ranch foreman. He was their boss, and they had trusted him. Then he had killed them both in cold blood. It couldn't have been anyone else.

Slocum cursed himself again for being so thickheaded, for not having seen through Rance right from the beginning. It had been Rance who'd had him arrested in the first place, who had been so adamant about having him charged with Ziggie's murder. Only when Marla had defended Slocum had Rance seemed to ease off and come around. But how the hell would he tell Marla? What proof did he have? He couldn't think of any. And Marla was sweet on Rance. Anyone could see that.

He decided to think on it for a while, and in the meantime, take care of things that were more immediate. There were two good cowboys who needed decent burials. He would see to that. Then he would decide how to deal with Rance. He had to find something with which to dig, for he had no shovel. The graves would be shallow, so he would have to cover them with rocks to protect the bodies from predators. It was a distasteful business, and Slocum found himself hating the no-good bastard who was responsible for it all.

At last the job was done. Slocum stood awhile beside the two fresh graves, holding his hat in his hands. He couldn't think of anything to say. At last, he put his hat on and turned away. He was thinking about riding back to the ranch, but he was afraid that he would see Rance, and he did not know if he would be able to control himself. He would like to just kill the bastard, but he knew that he couldn't do that. There was not only Marla to convince of his guilt. There was Burl Johnson. While he was standing there thinking it over, he looked at the wagon load of silver ore, and he had a thought.

It took just a little while for Slocum to round up the wagon horses, and even less time to hitch them back to the wagon. He tied his Appaloosa to the tailgate and climbed into the seat. He didn't really have any particular destination in mind. He just wanted to move the wagon. He drove straight ahead in the canyon. Then he saw a small wash off to the side. There wasn't much to it. No one would even look for it. He drove the wagon in there and turned the horses loose again. Then he mounted up and rode back out. He looked around for something he could use to wipe out the wagon tracks. This might do the trick. It might just cause a falling out among thieves, and when that happened, Slocum would be right there watching.

16

Over in Complacency, Mac Sowles was wrapped in a blanket in his jail cell. He and the locked-up miners grumbled at each other back and forth in the two adjacent cells. It was about mid-morning when Rod Fields came walking into the sheriff's office with the mayor.

"Boyd," said Sowles, "get me my britches over there and unlock this damn cell. That fucking Slocum put me in here like this. I got to get on his trail. The son of a bitch."

"Mac, I deputized Slocum. You're in there charged with conspiring with Charlie Dode and all these other men who are locked up here. I'm putting Rod, here, in charge temporarily till we can call a new election, so just calm down."

The mayor walked over to the other side of the office and picked up Sowles's britches. He went to the jail cell and poked them through the bars. Sowles grabbed them up and struggled into them with the blanket still wrapped around his shoulders. Once he had on his britches, he tossed the blanket aside.

"Well, give me the rest of my clothes, will you?"

Rod looked at the mayor, who nodded his head, and then he fetched over the clothes. In another minute, Sowles was dressed again. "Now," he said, "what the hell is this all about? Just what are you accusing me of anyhow?"

"You heard me the first time, Mac," said the mayor. "Just

keep quiet. Rodney's in charge here now, and I've got work to do back over at my office. Rod, if you need anything, just holler. You know where to find me."

"Yes sir," said Rod, as the mayor left the office.

"Rodney, you son of a bitch, open this cell door right now," growled Sowles. "I'm the sheriff here, duly elected, and you know that."

"I'm sorry, Mr. Sowles," said Rod, "but you heard the mayor. There ain't nothing I can do."

"Goddamn it," said Sowles. He began pacing the floor and mumbling to himself. The miners next door were also talking among themselves, grumbling and complaining. Sowles began to think that when Rod brought them something to eat, they could jump him, but when the time came, Rod brought Dave Scott with him to hold a shotgun, and he made them all move to the far wall until he had put all the trays in the cells and locked the doors again. Sowles began to think that his situation was hopeless. He was afraid that he would actually have to stand trial.

It looked like Charlie Dode had run out on him too, him and all the others. Charlie Dode was a skunk. He had enough money squirreled away that he had stolen from the Circle Z mine, he could afford to hire the best lawyer around, but Sowles was beginning to believe that Dode was long gone with all the money.

"Hey, Mac," said one of the miners. "What the hell are we going to do?"

"Shit," said Sowles, "how the hell should I know. We just got to watch for an opportunity here. That's all I can say."

"But Rod never opens a cell door but what he's got that other feller there holding that damn shotgun."

"Well, there you have it. I don't know no more than you do."

It was time for supper, and Rod left the office. Sowles was still pacing the floor. Most of the miners were sitting on the cots or on the floor. The grumbling had stopped. Everyone was tired, and no one could think of anything more to say.

Sowles had paced over to the window and turned away from it to pace the other direction when he heard something fall to the floor behind him. He turned quickly. He did not see anyone at the window. He looked down to spy a Moore .32-caliber revolver on the floor. He grabbed it up fast and checked it. It was fully loaded. Keeping his back to the cell door, he tucked it under his shirt.

"Mac," said a miner.

"Shut up," said Sowles.

In another few minutes, Rod and Dave came back with the trays. They put the trays on the desk, and Dave headed for the gun rack to get the shotgun. Sowles pulled out the revolver and pointed it through the bars.

"If you get any closer to that shotgun," he said, "you're a dead man."

Dave stopped and looked over his shoulder. He looked from the gun barrel to Rod. Rod was looking at the gun and not moving.

"Rod?" said Dave.

"Just be still," said Rod.

"That's smart," said Sowles. "Now fetch them keys over here and unlock the door."

"What if I don't do that, Mac?" said Rod. "You going to kill us and still be locked up in there? Then they'll have you for murder."

"I'll tell you one thing, Rod," Sowles said. "If you don't do like I say, I'll kill you right now, and then I betcha ole Dave'll fetch the keys on over. Won't you, Dave?"

"Rod," said Dave, "I don't care if they hang him. If he shoots me first, I'll be dead. It won't matter to me. I'm sorry, Rod." He walked over to the peg on the wall and grabbed the keys that were hanging there. Then he unlocked the cell door, and Sowles stepped out quickly shoving him toward the other cell.

"Let them out," he ordered.

Dave opened the other door, and the sheriff shoved Dave inside. Then the miners rushed on Rod, disarmed him and shoved him in with Dave. They shut the door and locked it and tossed the keys across the room.

"Arm yourselves, boys," said Sowles.

The men rushed over to the gun cabinet and grabbed rifles, shotguns, and revolvers. Sowles did the same. "All right," he said, "you men go on down to the stable and get horses for us all. Then bring them back here ready to ride. If anyone tries to stop you, kill him."

"Just like that?" asked one of the miners.

"We've done burned all our bridges here," Sowles answered. "Get going."

The miners hurried out to do as they'd been told while Sowles pulled out desk drawers and stuffed his pockets with any personal possessions he had stashed there.

"Mac," said Rod, "you're making a big mistake. If you stay here, you might could beat the charges in court."

"I don't think so," Sowles said. He walked over to the door to look out on the street. "Come on," he said. "Come on." At last he saw the miners coming, all mounted and leading an extra horse. "See you boys around," he said, and he hurried outside and climbed on the horse's back. A little ways down the street, he stopped at the bank. "A couple of you boys come inside with me," he said.

Three miners dismounted and went into the bank with him. A teller looked up as they came in. "Yes, sir, Sheriff," he said, "what can I do for you today?"

Apparently the word had not yet spread. "I want to make a withdrawal," Sowles said. "Give me all my money. While you're at it, you might just as well give me all the cash you got."

"What?"

"You heard me. Lay it all out on the counter."

In another few minutes Sowles and the other three men, pockets stuffed with bills, went back outside and mounted up. As they turned their horses to ride out of town, Sowles saw the mayor stepping out of his office.

"Hey," Mayor Hager called.

Sowles turned in his saddle and fired one shot, dropping

the mayor in his tracks. Then, "Come on, boys," he called out, and they rode hard out of town. A couple of miles out, they slowed their horses, and one of the miners said, "Mac, where are we going?"

"I got an idea where Charlie Dode is holed up," Sowles said. "Let's slip up on that bastard."

They rode on a few more miles before the man said, "What will we do, Mac?"

"I ain't decided yet. He's got a bunch of money and a wagon load of silver hid out somewhere. Trying to hold out on us."

"Well, who dropped that gun in the window for you?"

"I don't know," Sowles said. "I don't think Charlie done it though. He wouldn't show his ass in town, the chicken-shit."

"No, but likely he sent Chance or Jonsey. I reckon they're still with him."

"Maybe. We'll see."

"Well, who else could it a been?"

"I don't know, damn it. We'll just have to wait and see, won't we?"

Rance walked up to the front door of the Circle Z ranch house and knocked. He waited impatiently, and he was about to open the door and walk on in, when Marla answered. "Rance," she said. "Come on in." He stepped brusquely past her, and she closed the door. When she turned around, Rance was right there, blocking her path. "Let's move over there and sit down," she said.

"Marla," said Rance, "I want an answer to my question."

"Not here," she said, "and not now."

"What's wrong with here and now?"

"Hettie and Burl are just in the next room," she said, her voice low.

"All right," he said. "Let's step out onto the porch."

Marla turned, opened the door and went outside. Rance followed her. She took a chair, and he did too. "Well?" he said.

"Rance, there's just too much happening right now. I can't think straight."

"What's to think about? You know how long I've been around here, running this ranch for your daddy and now for you. We're fighting all the fights together. And the way things have been between us, why not just go on and do it? Say yes, Marla. Let's get married right away."

"There's a lot of preparation for a wedding," Marla said. "Right now, I don't have time to plan. Just be patient a little longer. Let's get all this settled. What's your hurry anyway?"

"I'm tired of sneaking around, Marla. I want everyone to know about us. I'm not ashamed to tell the world that I love you."

"Oh, Rance," she said. "Not yet."

Rance stood up angrily and paced away. He turned back to look at Marla. "Not yet," he said. "Not yet. When then?"

"I told you, Rance. When we've settled all this trouble."

He went back to his chair and sat down, still disgusted. "All right," he said. "I'll wait a little longer, but not much."

Marla sat thinking for a moment in silence. There had been a question nagging at her for some time, and she decided that it was time to ask. "Rance," she said, "how long have you known Charlie Dode?"

"What?"

"How long have you known him?"

"A few months," he said. "Since he came to work here at the mine. Why?"

"That's funny," she said.

"What? What's wrong?"

"Well, I was going through some of Daddy's papers the other day," she said.

"Yeah?"

"I found a note he had written that said you had recommended that he hire Charlie."

"What? Oh, yeah. I can see how that might give you the wrong impression. Ziggie was checking into several different men, looking for a mine boss, you know. He showed me the credentials of them, and he asked my opinion. That's all."

"Oh, I see."

"Is that all that's been holding you up? Listen, Marla—"

He stopped when he saw Slocum approaching from the corral, and under his breath, he muttered, "Damn." Slocum walked up to the porch and stopped at the bottom step.

"Howdy," he said, touching the brim of his hat. "Am I interrupting anything?"

"Not at all, Slocum," Marla said. "Come on up and join us."

"Thanks." He mounted the stairs and pulled up a chair, sitting near Marla. He knew what he was doing, and he could see that it was working. He was rankling Rance, and Rance was trying to cover it up, but he was not doing a very good job of it. Rance squirmed a little, and then stood up.

"Well, I've got work to do around this place," he said. "Unlike some others."

He stomped down the stairs and stalked off toward the corral. "What was all that about?" Slocum asked.

"Oh, nothing much," said Marla, "but I'm glad you came."

Slocum took a cigar out of his pocket and lit it. "Sounds to me like it was about something," he said.

"You're right," she said. "Oh, Rance has been after me to marry him."

"And you don't want to?"

"I don't know, Slocum. He's been here for so long, working for Daddy, and now for me. He knows this ranch better than anyone else."

"Is that a reason to get hitched to a feller?"

"No," she said. "I don't believe it is, but Rance is insistent."

"It ain't so hard to say no."

"There's something else," Marla said. "I've been trying to explain it away. I even asked him about it, and he did explain it. Sort of."

Slocum waited a moment, and then he said, "You want to tell me about it?"

"I found a note where Daddy wrote down that Rance had recommended he hire Charlie Dode to run the mine."

"And you confronted Rance with that information?"

"Yeah. I did."

"What'd he say?"

"Well, first off, I asked him how long he had known Charlie, and he said just since Charlie came to work at the mine. Then I told him about the note, and he hesitated a little, and then he said that he'd looked over Charlie's credentials."

"That's it?"

"Yeah. But I don't like it, Slocum."

"Well, I don't either, and I'll tell you why. When we rode out to the mine the other morning, we found it abandoned. There was one feller out there. Everyone else was gone."

"Yeah. I know that."

"I figure someone went out there and warned them that we was coming."

"Rance?"

"It could easily have been Rance."

Marla didn't say anything, but she recalled that Rance had stood her up the night before. She felt her face burn.

"Then when I sent those two boys back here with that wagon," Slocum said, "they never showed up. I went back out there and trailed the wagon. Someone met them and changed their course. They went out to a blind canyon, unhitched the horses, and then whoever it was that had met them shot them both in the back."

"Oh, God, Slocum, you don't think—"

"I told those boys to bring the wagon here," Slocum said. "Who could've changed the orders and had them go along like that? It was someone they trusted, Marla. I can't think of no one else it could be."

17

"Slocum," Marla said, "what should we do?"

"I'd say that depends on you."

"On me," she said, and she sounded faraway.

"Are you convinced?"

"Slocum, if we're right, that means that Rance had my daddy killed."

"Maybe. Could be that Charlie Dode or even Tobe could've made that decision by himself. I don't think we'll ever know for sure."

"Even if Charlie Dode made the decision, if Rance is in on the whole thing, has been all along, then he'd have made that same decision if he'd been there."

"That's likely."

"Kill him, Slocum," she said.

"I can't do that, Marla. Now that ole Burl has made me a deputy, I'll have to just go and arrest him. We'll have to let the law handle it from there."

"All right, all right. Go on out there and arrest him then, but I don't think he'll go with you. I think he'll resist, and you'll have to kill him just the same."

"If it happens that way, then it'll be his doing, not mine."

Slocum stood up to leave.

"You going after Rance?"

"Yes, ma'am," he said. "That's what you want, ain't it?"

Marla sat quiet for a moment. Then she said, "Yes. Go after him."

Sowles and his band of renegade miners and bank robbers rode up to a line shack on the far reaches of the Circle Z Ranch, but they saw no horses there. They stopped and sat still in their saddles for a moment. Then Sowles got down off his horse and walked to the door, kicking it open. He went inside, looked around a bit, then walked back out.

"Ain't no one here," he said, walking back to his horse. He climbed back into the saddle.

"What do we do now?" asked one of the gang.

"Well, we got to find Charlie," Sowles said, "but that ain't all. There's that Slocum. He'll be interfering all the way unless he's killed first. Besides that, I owe him for something. Let's head down toward the Circle Z ranch house and find that damn Slocum."

"And kill him?"

"Hell, yes, we'll kill the son of a bitch. Come on."

Rance had stalked away from the ranch house in a heavy pout, and Slocum had made the big mistake of not watching which way the man went. He had gone to the corral for a horse, that much Slocum knew. Beyond that was a mystery. It shouldn't be too much trouble to find him. He did not know yet that Slocum was on to him. Of course, Marla had tipped her hand a bit when she asked about ole Ziggie's note, but that shouldn't have been enough to really alert Rance that they were on to him. Slocum tried to read the tracks leaving the corral, but there was no way. There were far too many of them.

He rode to the bunkhouse, but there was no sign of Rance around there. The man was gone. Slocum reasoned that if he had been in that same position, he would likely head for the nearest saloon. That was the Hognose in Rascality. Then he chuckled. He had been in that same position not too long ago. He had left the Circle Z in a big pout, and he had gone to the Hognose Saloon. That was the beginning of his getting himself involved in this whole mess. He thought about that as he rode toward town.

He told himself if he had not gotten involved, Dode and Rance would have the whole ranch by this time, and likely Rance would be married to Marla. She would have been tricked into believing that he had saved the day for her. Likely that had been his plan all along. He guessed that it had all been for the best. He thought about Marla telling him to go out and kill Rance, and he knew what she had been thinking. She had been thinking that she had allowed the slimy bastard into her bed. Slocum was sure of that. He didn't blame her. He wanted to kill Rance.

He was maybe halfway to town when he saw the large group of riders coming toward him. He did not recognize any of them at first, but he was curious about so large a group of men riding together across the prairie. They weren't moving too fast, not at first. But they came closer, still headed for him, and he recognized Mac Sowles. At the same instant, the gang started riding hard and fast for him. Slocum looked around.

There was no way he could make it to town ahead of them. He might get back to the ranch, but he did not want to bring such a bunch to the unprotected ranch house. The crew was all out on the range somewhere. There was only one thing to do. He turned the big Appaloosa toward the abandoned mine and kicked it into a fast run. He heard bullets behind him as he raced toward the mine. He looked back over his shoulder to see the pursuit coming. They were a bunch of fools. They were too far back for revolver shots, so they were just wasting their ammunition. He kept going at full speed, not wanting to let them get any closer.

Now and then, he looked back to make sure, but he felt safe. He was putting a little more distance between himself and the gang of outlaws. The horses they were riding could not begin to keep up with his. He kept going, kept up the pace. Glancing back again, he saw that he had plenty of space between, so he suddenly stopped the Appaloosa.

"Sit still, pard," he said to his horse as he slipped the Winchester out of the scabbard. The horse obeyed. Slocum cranked a shell into the chamber and raised the rifle to his shoulder. He took aim and squeezed off a shot. One of the miners dropped from his saddle, and the others hauled back on their reins. They milled around a bit, turned and rode back to a safe distance. Slocum put the rifle away and rode for the mine again. He had one less pursuer to worry about. He looked back again. They were still coming, but they were deliberately hanging back now. That was good. That would give him more time to get situated at the mine.

He showed no mercy for the Appaloosa. He ran it hard the rest of the way. When he at last reached the mine, he rode past the stairway that led up to the office. Instead, he rode his horse right up the side of the hill to the mine entrance. When he reached the entrance, he dismounted, pulling out the Winchester again, and he slapped the Appaloosa on the rump, sending it inside the mine. He wanted it safe from any mean-spirited shots that would come his way. Then he too went inside the mine, but just inside. He leaned against the upright post that served to brace one side of the entrance, and he cranked another shell into the chamber of his rifle. He waited.

He looked down on the approaching gang of outlaws, as Sowles held up a hand to stop them. He watched as they sat there, apparently discussing the situation. He was in the same position as had been the man abandoned by Charlie Dode. He had the advantage in terms of position and vantage point, but he was far outnumbered. He felt sure that Mac Sowles knew all that too. Well, the next move was up to them.

The next move was theirs, but they didn't make a move. Instead, they dismounted. He watched, as they took drinks of water, or whatever they had in their canteens. Some of them lit cigarettes or cigars. Some sat down on the ground and relaxed. They were too far out for a shot, even with his Winchester. He wondered what the hell they were pulling. Then it came to him. They were waiting for dark. They were planning to sneak up close under cover of darkness.

Well, Slocum decided, two could play that game. He stepped out of the mine entrance so he could be plainly seen, and he took out a cigar and lit it. Then he sat down to smoke. He tried to think about what he would do when they finally started to move in on him. It was no good to hope for rescue from the cowhands at the Circle Z. There was no reason for any of them to be riding out this direction. The cattle were over on the other side of the ranch. No one knew that he had come out here either. It would be up to him. By himself.

There were six outlaws still down there with Sowles, after Slocum had killed one. It was one against seven. After dark, they could spread out and be coming at him from all directions. The sky was cloudy, and unless a friendly wind came up to blow them over, he would get no help from stars or moon that night. He would have to rely a lot on his hearing, and he would have to be listening very carefully for any sound of approach. He considered that he could easily die that night on the side of that mountain. The thought of death did not bother him nearly so much as the thought of Mac Sowles alive and gloating over it.

He itched to raise the rifle and try another shot, but he knew that it would be no use. The distance was too great. Almost absentmindedly, he looked over toward the mine office. And then he recalled the old rifle in the corner. The Sharps. He looked out at the outlaws, and he considered the range of the buffalo gun. He could pick them off easy with that thing, if it would work at all. He remembered the layer of dust that covered the old gun, and he wondered how long it had been since anyone used it. He wondered if there was any ammunition for it. Well, there was only one way to find out.

There was no way to get to the office from the mine shaft without first going down to the bottom of the mountain, walking over and climbing the stairs. Slocum stood up and looked out at the gang, then started down. He noticed some activity out there when he did. They had a moment of panic, wondering what he was up to, but Sowles soon settled them down again. He could tell that they were watching him though, as he reached the bottom and walked toward the stairs.

Slocum stopped at the bottom of the stairs and looked back. Two of the outlaws stepped forward, but they stopped when Sowles said something to them. All of them were standing and looking in his direction. He climbed the stairs and looked back at them again from the landing before going on inside. He saw right away that the Sharps was still in the corner. He walked over and picked up the old gun. Then he pulled a chair up next to the window. He sat where he could watch the outlaw gang, and he examined the Sharps. It had been sadly neglected, but it was a fine old weapon. And it was loaded.

Slocum took a handkerchief out of his pocket and dusted the gun off. Then he tried the works. Amazingly, everything was smooth. But he had only one shot. He could use it to take out Sowles. With Sowles out of the way, the rest of the fools would run around not knowing what the hell to do. He decided that it would be worth a try. A Sharps was usually used with a tripod, but Slocum had the window ledge. It would do. He raised the gun up and laid it on the ledge. Then he put his shoulder to it. He looked through the sight for Mac Sowles, and he found him. It was a long shot, but the Sharps was up to it, and so was Slocum.

He squeezed the trigger, and just as he did, one of the outlaws stepped in front of Sowles. An instant later the lead from the Sharps tore into the man's back. Slocum could see the blood spurt onto Sowles from his perch in the mine office. He saw the man jerk and fall. He watched as Sowles and the others all jumped up and ran back. He could hear their shouts. He put the now useless Sharps aside and took up his Winchester again. The outlaws mounted up rode out in both directions to the side.

Sowles had decided that, because of that rifle shot, they couldn't wait till dark. He had no way of knowing that Slocum had no more bullets for the gun he had just used. Slocum watched carefully as the fanned out gang moved in closer, and when he saw one within the range of his Winchester, he picked him off. He narrowed them down to five. Things were looking a little better.

He went outside and hurried down the stairs, then ran along the foot of the mountain to the place that led up to the mine. Three shots rang out, but none of them reached him. The distance was still too great. He made it back up to the mine entrance and ducked inside. From there, his view of the outlaws was pretty good. He looked to the right, and he saw a man moving along close to the base of the mountain, a rifle in his hands. He was approaching the stairs from the other side. Slocum took aim and fired, but his bullet only kicked up dirt near the man's head. The outlaw turned and crawfished.

"Damn," said Slocum. He had wasted his first shot.

Suddenly, three men started shooting from his left, and the bullets came too close for comfort. Slocum ducked into the mine entrance for safety. In another minute, the shooting stopped. He decided to move farther into the mine. Along the way, he took the big stallion a little farther back for safety. Then he squatted down next to the wall on his left and waited. Anyone looking into the mine would not be able to see him in the darkness, but they would be silhouetted there in the entrance for him.

For several minutes, everything was quiet. Then a man stepped into the entrance. He was a fool. Slocum started to shoot, but he waited. Let them try to figure things out. The man twisted and turned as if he were trying to see into the darkness, and then a second man appeared by his side. There were only four left. Four and Sowles. Slocum decided that the time was right. He raised the Winchester to his shoulder and fired, cranking another shell into the chamber at once, to raise the rifle and fire again.

The first shot dropped the first man, and the other turned to run. The second shot tore into his back. Then everything got quiet again. It was a waiting game. Sowles and two more men were outside. Would they wait for Slocum to show himself at the mine entrance, or would they grow impatient and come up looking for him? After what had happened to the last two, he thought they would not show themselves to him in that way. It was a standoff, it seemed.

Slocum's legs were going to sleep, so he stood up to stretch. He decided to walk around, and he walked farther back into the mine. It was dark, and he couldn't see anything, so he moved slowly. Then he walked into the wall. He stopped and dug a match out of his pocket. Striking the match, he saw that the tunnel made a sharp right turn. His match was about to go out, but he saw a lantern on the wall, so he lit it. He took the lantern and walked farther.

He had gone a pretty good distance before he began to wonder what the three outlaws outside were doing. He was about to decide that he was wasting his time when he saw the light. It wasn't much. A small hole. He moved ahead. In a few minutes, he was standing before a tiny exit, just big enough to crawl through. It might have been put there on purpose for an emergency exit, or it might have simply appeared there by accident. Slocum decided, though, that its appearance was good luck to him. He blew out the light in the lantern and crawled up to peer out of the hole.

Looking out, he could see that he was well behind the three surviving outlaws. He could see them where they were hunkered down for safety, looking up toward the mine. Carefully, he poked his arm holding the Winchester through the hole, then followed with his head. It wasn't easy, but in a couple of minutes, he had wriggled through. He was on the outside, sitting on the edge of the mountain. There was no trail. No path. And he was exposed, if anyone would turn around and look.

He was within rifle range too, and he thought about taking a shot, but rejected that thought. There were three of them down there. He could easily have hit one, but the other two would have time to duck for cover. Then they would have clear shots at him. It was not a good idea. Slocum looked down the side of the mountain, wondering if he could make his way down there safely, quietly, and undetected. Sowles and the other two had all their attention on the mine entrance, but all it would take was one turn of the head. His only other choice was to go back the way he had come and resume the standoff. He decided to go down.

He would have to move slowly and carefully. One slip would create a small slide, not enough to cause Slocum any trouble, but enough to make the outlaws look around. He had to keep his eyes on where he was going, but he had to keep watching the three outlaws as well. It was a tricky business, but he had made up his mind. He started down. He stopped still once when Sowles straightened up and seemed to look around, but the crooked sheriff did not look in his direction. He kept going.

He was about halfway down, when his foot slipped, sending dozens of small rocks rolling down the side of the mountain. He looked down at first, but then quickly he looked in the direction of the outlaws. They had seen him. He might be able to stop himself, but it would take time, and they would have good shots at him. He decided to go all the way to the bottom. He slid and he rolled, and he heard the shots as the outlaws tried to hit him. When he landed at the bottom, he rolled some more, and then came up to his feet.

He brought the Winchester to his shoulder and fired a shot. One outlaw screamed and went down. Sowles and the other one disappeared behind some boulders. Slocum got down flat on the ground. He heard some running, and he stood up to run after them. When he spotted them, Sowles was out in front, going for a horse. Slocum raised his rifle again, but the other outlaw stopped running, turned and fired a wild shot. Slocum dropped him in his tracks, but Sowles was mounted up and riding away fast. Slocum fired two shots after him, but they both went wide. He ran back up into the mine for his horse. By the time he had brought it out, there was no sign of Sowles on the horizon, and the sun was low in the west.

Slocum sat down for a breather. It had been a long day, and he was tired. He thought about what had just happened, and he calculated what was left to do. Sowles had to be run down. And there was Charlie Dode. Likely there were still two miners with him. Last but not least, there was Rance. It no longer mattered to Slocum who he went after next. They were all guilty, and he knew it. So did Marla and Burl Johnson. He would just go looking and take whatever came up in his way.

18

Slocum made up his mind that whichever of the three he ran into first, he was going to give one warning and then start shooting. He had fooled around with this long enough. He decided to ride back to the ranch and see if by any chance ole Rance was still fool enough to be hanging around. He could check in on Burl Johnson too while he was at it. After that, he didn't know. Maybe he would ride into Rascality just in case any of the three dared to show themselves in there. He wasn't sure. There was sure a lot of open space around for three men to hide in, and there was only one reason to expect any of them to still be around. That was the ore wagon.

It was dark before he made it back to the ranch house. He put away his horse for the night and walked over to the big house. He was about to knock on the front door when Marla opened it from the inside.

"Saw you coming," she said. "Come on in."

Slocum walked in, taking off his hat. He was pleased to see Burl Johnson sitting in one of the big comfortable chairs. He walked over and shook hands with Johnson.

"You must be doing some better," he said.

"I'll fight you tomorrow," said Johnson.

"I'm afraid you'd whip me," Slocum said.

"Did Doc say anything about whiskey?" Marla asked.

160

"I don't recall that he did," said Johnson.

"What do you say we all have us a drink?"

"Sounds good to me," said Slocum. "Say, where's Hettie?"

"She said she was fixing to change the sheets in there," said Johnson.

Bottle in hand, Marla walked over to the door to the bedroom where Johnson was staying. Poking her head in, she said, "You want to have a little drink with us, Hettie?"

"I don't mind if I do," Hettie said. "Thanks. I'll be right out."

By the time Marla had the four glasses poured, Hettie was out of the bedroom. Marla distributed the glasses. "Do we have anything good to drink to?" she said.

"I'd say so," said Slocum. "For one thing, we got ole Burl's good health."

"Here, here," said Johnson.

"Then all that mess we been dealing with is all straightened out. Everyone's dead except for the main three, and they sure ain't operating no more. I'll get them sooner or later, if they don't leave the country first."

"Slow down, Slocum," said Johnson. "What main three are you talking about?"

"Well, there's Charlie Dode," Slocum said, "and then there's that damn sheriff from over at Complacency, ole Mac Sowles. He's out loose."

"He break jail?" said Johnson.

"Him and all the others that was in over there. They jumped me out on the road. I killed them all but Sowles. He got away clean."

"You killed them all?" said Johnson. "How many?"

"Hell, I forget. Six or seven. Oh, something else I forgot. I expect that ole Dode's got a couple of them bastards still with him."

"Is there any chance they skipped the country?" Marla said.

"There's always a chance," Slocum said, "but there's also that wagon load of ore that I sent back here. My guess is that them three are looking for it. And maybe for each other. Then there's ole Rance. Have you seen Rance around today?"

"I haven't seen Rance since he stomped off the porch," said Marla.

"Well, Rance is most likely going to be the easiest one to get hold of," Slocum said, "on account of he don't know we're onto him. He stomped outa here because of me. That's all. He didn't like being interrupted."

Hettie and Johnson looked at each other. "Are we missing something here?" Johnson asked.

"No," said Marla. "Not much anyhow. Rance has been after me to marry him. That's all."

"Oh."

"I'm more like to kill him. The son of a bitch."

"Remember what I told you, Marla," Johnson said.

"Yeah. All right."

Slocum made him a place near the corral to sleep that night, thinking that Rance just might come on back to the ranch. He had quite a stake in the place, and he was after a right smart prize in Marla. He had no reason to believe that Slocum was suspicious of him either, so he had no real reason to stay away. Slocum kept his clothes on. He just snugged down inside a blanket to keep warm.

It was around midnight when something woke him up. He was careful not to make any quick moves. He opened his eyes and looked toward the corral. He saw someone opening the gate to take a horse in. Whoever it was was in the corral with the horse for a few minutes, taking care of the horse probably. Finally, a lone figure came back through the gate and closed the gate behind himself. Slocum watched as the man walked toward the big house. There were no lights on in the house. It was not the time for anyone to come calling.

Slocum carefully laid the blanket aside, as he watched the man move toward the house. He stood up and started to follow, slowly, and he slid the Colt out of the holster at his side. As he followed, the man walked around the big house, going to the back. Slocum kept after him until he saw the man start to rap on a window. He moved in a little closer and waited. The window opened, and he heard Marla's voice.

"Rance! What the hell do you want here?"

"Don't you know? We were interrupted before. We need to finish what we were talking about. I'm coming in."

Rance reached for the windowsill, but Marla said, "Rance. Go away."

"What for?" he said. "We need to talk."

"I got one thing to say to you, Rance," said Marla. "You're fired. Pack up your things and get out. Now!"

Slocum decided that it was time for him to make his move, so he raised the revolver and thumbed back the hammer. "I got something to say to you too, Rance," he said. "You're under arrest."

Rance slapped leather, and Slocum squeezed his trigger. Rance's gun was out, but it was still pointed at the ground when Slocum's bullet smashed into his chest. It was high, though, and on the right side. Blood poured out of the fresh wound, staining the front of Rance's shirt. Rance dropped his gun. He staggered and fell against the side of the house.

"Oh," he said. "Oh, God. You've killed me, you son of a bitch."

Slocum walked over for a better look. He pulled Rance's hand away from the wound. It was ugly, but Slocum did not figure it was fatal.

"You ain't that lucky," he said. "You come with me. Marla, will you let us in the front door?"

With Hettie's help, Slocum patched up the hole he had put in Rance's chest. Then he tied Rance's arms, just to make sure the ex-foreman did not try to pull anything on them in the night. Rance grumbled and complained, but Slocum ignored him.

"What do you mean to do with him?" Johnson asked.

"First thing in the morning," said Slocum, "I mean to take him to town and lock him in jail."

"That's good, Slocum," said Johnson.

"What the hell am I under arrest for?" said Rance.

"Conspiracy," said Johnson. "Conspiring with Charlie Dode to steal from this ranch. We'll detail it all for you later."

"You got no proof."

"If Slocum's shot had been better," said Marla, "we wouldn't need any. Damn it."

"I think we got enough for any jury around here to convict with," Slocum said. "You just shut up. Try to sleep. You'll need it come morning."

The following morning, they had breakfast, and then Slocum loaded Rance on a horse and headed for Rascality with him. "You won't prove anything on me, Slocum," Rance said.

"That ain't my job."

"I'll be out, and I'll heal up. I'll get you for this, you son of a bitch."

"You can try."

"I know you're a hell of a gunfighter, Slocum, and I ain't, but I ain't ashamed to slip up behind a man neither. See, if the tables was turned right now, if I had you where you have me, you'd never show up at the jail alive. That's where I got the advantage on you, Slocum. One of these days, I'll kill you. I'll kill you for what you messed up for me. I almost had the ranch and Marla. I would have, if you hadn't come along."

"The joke's on you, Rance. It was you that kept me here when you accused me of killing Ziggie. I'd a been outa here the next morning. You'd have never seen me again. You'd be up here having your own crooked-ass way."

"You son of a bitch. I'll get you. I will."

Slocum spent the rest of that day, after having deposited Rance in the jail and notifying Doc of the prisoner's condition, talking to various officials in Rascality. With a note he carried in from Burl Johnson, he was able to get the town to hire a deputy to watch over the jail. "I'm just temporary," he told them. "I ain't even on the payroll." Once he had all his business taken care of, he stopped by the Hognose for a drink, and Rowdy came by to sit with him.

"Haven't seen you around, stranger," she said.

"I been pretty busy, Rowdy. Have a drink with me."

"Don't mind if I do," she said.

Slocum poured another drink for Rowdy. She took a sip and gave him a fetching look. "You, uh, wanta go upstairs with me?"

"That would sure be a lot of fun," he said, "but I just stopped in for a drink. I've got things I got to be doing."

"Like what?"

"I'm looking for a couple of men," Slocum said.

"Sounds serious. What do you mean to do when you find them?"

"Either kill them or put them in jail. That part's up to them."

"Anyone I know?"

Slocum shrugged. "One of them used to be the sheriff over at Complacency. Name's Mac Sowles."

"Never heard of him," Rowdy said. She took another drink.

"You might know ole Charlie Dode," said Slocum. "He used to run the Circle Z mine for ole Ziggie."

"Yeah," she said. "I know Charlie. The son of a bitch."

"How come you to call him that?"

"He's been in here," she said.

Slocum could tell that Rowdy did not really want to talk about Dode, but she had opened her mouth, and now he was curious.

"Tell me about it," he said.

"Ain't much to tell."

"Come on, Rowdy. Tell me."

"Let's just say he likes to hurt girls. Is that enough?"

"If that's all you want to tell me," Slocum said, "then that's enough. Somehow I'm not surprised to hear that. You haven't seen him lately, have you?"

"He's been in."

"Recent?"

"Couple of nights ago. I didn't go up with him though. I made myself scarce when I seen him come in. I ain't stupid enough to go for that shit twice."

"He ain't staying here in town, is he?"

"I wouldn't know about that," Rowdy said, "but I would say he ain't far away."

"Rowdy, girl," said Slocum, "you've just given me one more reason to run that no-good son of a bitch down. When I take him, one way or the other, I'll think about you."

"When you take that bastard, you come on over here and let me know, will you? You and me will go upstairs and stay for the whole night, and there won't be no charge neither."

Slocum smiled and patted her hand. "I'll be looking forward to that," he said.

Charlie Dode, Chance, and one more miner known as Scar, because of an ugly streak across one cheek, rode cautiously up to the abandoned mine office. For a moment they sat silent in their saddles.

"There's still a plenty silver in there," Dode said at last. "It's a damn shame to have to ride away from it."

"When we riding away, Charlie?" Chance asked.

"Just as soon as we find that last wagon load of ore," Dode said. "It's around here somewhere."

"How you know it's still around?" asked Scar.

"Because it never made it over to Complacency," said Dode. "That's how come."

"Where could it be?"

"That's what we've got to find out. Did you see anything in town this morning?"

"I didn't see no wagon load of ore," Scar said. "Didn't see nothing too interesting. That Slocum feller brought in Rance from out to the Circle Z. Looked like he was shot."

"Rance? Shot?"

"Yeah."

"Why didn't you tell me about this, stupid?"

"It didn't seem important, I guess," Scar said.

"What did Slocum do with Rance?"

"Locked him up in jail."

"Damn it," said Dode. "So Slocum figured out that Rance was part of this operation."

"Rance was?" asked Chance.

"You heard me."

"I never knew that."

"No one was supposed to know it. I been wanting to have a talk with ole Rance, but I couldn't figure how to get to him out at the ranch. I wonder if he knows anything about that damn wagon."

"Why would he know anything?" asked Scar.

"The wagon never got to Complacency, did it? That means somebody caught up with it and turned it around. Where the hell would they take it? Back to the ranch likely. Rance was our man at the ranch. He ought to know where the damn wagon is."

"Yeah," said Scar.

"He ought," said Chance. "What are we going to do?"

"We're going into Rascality tonight," Dode said. "We're going to have us a talk with Rance."

19

The new, temporary deputy on charge at the Rascality jail was dozing at Burl Johnson's desk. It was late. Nearly midnight. There were still customers in the Hognose, naturally, but by and large, the streets of Rascality were empty when Charlie Dode, Scar, and Chance rode into town on a backstreet. They stopped behind the jail and dismounted. Chance tried the back door and found it locked.

"Go around front and try that one," Dode said to Scar.

"What do I do if I find it unlocked?"

"Go in and open the back door, stupid."

"Okay."

Scar walked around the building. He looked up and down the street so surreptitiously that had anyone been out there to watch, that person would have been immediately suspicious of Scar. He tried the door and found it locked. He walked back around behind the jail.

"The door's locked," he said.

"Shit," said Dode.

"What do we do now?" asked Scar.

"Shut up and let me think," said Dode. "All right. Here's what we'll do. We'll all three go around front. Me and Chance will stand to the sides of the door, and you'll knock. When that dumb deputy answers the door, we'll move in on him. Keep him quiet. Disarm him. But no shooting. We don't want to wake up the whole damn town. You got it?"

"Yeah."

"Got it, Boss."

Dode led the way back to the front door. When they arrived there, he stepped to the left of the door and pointed for Chance to go to the right. Then he nodded at Scar, who puffed up his chest and rapped on the door. Nothing happened.

"Louder," said Dode.

Scar pounded on the door. In a minute, the door opened a crack, and the deputy peeped out, but Dode immediately shoved on the door, pushing it wide open. Dode and the other two men were inside in a panicked heartbeat. "What the hell?" the surprised deputy said.

"Shut up," said Dode.

Chance pulled out his revolver and clubbed the poor wretch over the head, once, twice, before he fell senseless to the floor. "Get his gun," said Dode. Chance got the gun. In the cell, Rance stood up.

"Charlie?" he said. "Get me out of here."

"We'll get you out," said Dode, going for the keys on the wall. "Scar, keep an eye on that deputy." He moved quickly to the cell and unlocked the door. "Come on, you raggedy-ass bastard," he said. "Let's get out of here."

Dode led the way to the back door and unlocked it. He shoved Rance through first, and then he went out.

"What about the deputy?" asked Scar.

"Leave him, dummy," said Dode. "Come on."

They hurried on over to their horses, and as Dode mounted up, he said, "Scar, take Rance with you on your horse."

They were all mounted quickly, and they turned their horses and rode out of town. In a few miles, Rance said, "Charlie, where are we going?"

"What do you care? We got you out of jail."

"Yeah, but—"

"We're just going a few more miles out. Relax."

True to his word, Charlie Dode turned off the main road

and led the way to a campsite by a small stream. They stopped there and dismounted. Rance groaned from his chest wound as he slid down off the horse.

"What's wrong, Rance?" Dode asked. "You hurt?"

"That fucking Slocum shot me," Rance said.

"Aw, that's too bad. Let me see."

It was too dark to really see, but Dode feigned interest and looked at the shoulder. Then he poked the wound with his finger. "Right there?" he said. "That where it hurts?"

"Ow," Rance complained. "Yeah, it hurts there. Don't do that."

"Rance," said Dode, "we're partners, ain't we?"

"Well, sure."

"I got a question to ask you."

"Sure. What is it?"

"I want to know what you did with that last load of ore."

"Why, I don't know what you're talking about. What load?"

"You come out to the mine and told us it was time to get out. Remember?"

"Sure."

"So we did. With one last wagon load. We rode to Complacency, but the wagon never showed up. Where is it, Rance?"

"How would I know? I wasn't even out there. You know that."

"Rance, you asshole, the only thing that could have happened to that wagon is that Slocum got it, in which case he took it back to the ranch and you know where it is, or you got it. Don't try to pull my leg."

"I'm telling you, Charlie—"

Dode suddenly punched Rance in the shoulder, and Rance screamed with the pain. "Where is it, you son of a bitch?" Dode shouted at him. He punched again, and Rance screamed again.

"Don't, Charlie," Rance said. "All right. All right. I'll tell you where it is."

"I knew you'd come around," Dode said. "Well?"

"There's a canyon over on the far side of the ranch. No one ever goes in there. I took it there."

"Let's go then," Dode said.

"Now?"

"Right now."

Slocum had just finished his breakfast in the big house at the Circle Z. Burl Johnson was sitting at the table and eating with the rest of them. Everyone was in pretty good spirits. Charlie Dode and two miners were still at large, as was Mac Sowles, but the main fight was over. Marla had named a new ranch foreman, and the work was going on. She decided to wait for all the legalities regarding bank accounts in Rascality and Complacency to be cleared up before she worried about reopening the mine. She would have to find a mine boss she could trust. Slocum finished his coffee and got up from the table.

"I'm going to take ole Harry with me," he said, "and ride out to that canyon where I left that wagon. Now that Rance is in jail, no one knows it's out there. Might as well bring it on in."

He saddled his Appaloosa and headed for the canyon with Harry riding alongside him. It was a long ride, and the day was mostly gone before they got there. The first thing Slocum noticed was fresh horse tracks. Then Harry saw the body of Rance. Slocum rode over to it and got off his horse to examine it, and he found that Rance's head had been beaten in with a rock. He scowled and stood up.

"Who done that, you reckon?" Harry asked.

"Someone must've busted Rance out of jail," said Slocum. "It could've been Dode or Sowles. My guess is it was Dode on account of the number of horses. He likely got Rance out to show him where he hid the silver ore, but poor ole Rance didn't know that I had come out here and moved it. They killed him for a double-crosser."

"How long ago, you reckon?"

"Not long," Slocum said. "My guess is we just missed them. Let's leave that wagon for a while and go after them."

"That's all right with me."

Slocum mounted up again, and they followed the tracks out of the canyon. They didn't seem to be headed anywhere in particular, and in a couple of hours, they disappeared. Slocum and Harry wasted another hour looking for them, but it was no use. "Hell," Slocum said, "let's go back and get the wagon. We've lost the trail."

They went back into the canyon, and Slocum led the way to the place he had tucked it away. It was still there, still loaded. It took a while, but they found the wagon horses and rounded them up. Then they hitched them to the wagon, tied Harry's horse on behind, and, with Harry driving the wagon, headed back for the ranch house. They were just coming out of the mouth of the canyon, when they saw that three riders blocked their way. The sun was behind the three, so they appeared as silhouettes. Harry stopped the wagon. Slocum sat beside it on his horse.

"Is that you, Dode?" Slocum called out.

"It's me, Slocum," Dode answered. "We seen you riding out this way, and I figured you were after that ore. We'll take it now."

"Don't be foolish, Dode," Slocum said. "Three against two ain't such bad odds."

"All three of us got rifles in our hands already, ready to shoot. We can knock you down before you can get yours out. You might could hit me with your six-gun from there, but I doubt it."

"Could you knock me down before I could kill these wagon horses?"

"What?"

"How would you get this wagon out of here if I was to kill the horses?"

"You wouldn't shoot them horses," Dode said.

"Why not?" Slocum slipped the Colt out and aimed at one of the horses. Following his lead, Harry did the same.

"Slocum," said Dode, his voice desperate, "don't do that."

"Then don't crowd me."

"All right, damn it, you win. We ain't shooting at you.

But just what the hell do you think you're going to do?"

"We're headed for the ranch house, Dode. There's plenty of cowhands there, and Sheriff Johnson. He's getting around pretty well by now. You want to ride along with us?"

"You ain't riding away from me with all that silver. That's for sure."

"Then start for the ranch."

Slocum nodded at Harry, and Harry flicked the reins. The horses started to pull, and the wagon rolled toward home. Dode and the other two riders moved out away from the wagon as it rolled toward them. Slocum kept his Colt in his hand and his eyes on Dode and his henchmen. "Hey, Dode," he called out.

"What?"

"In case you're thinking too hard out there, you'd ought to know that there ain't a man alive can handle my horse but me. So if me and Harry was to shoot these wagon horses, even if you shot us, you couldn't make my horse pull a wagon. Harry's wouldn't be able to do it alone."

"Damn you, Slocum."

"Just thought I'd mention it."

"It's still a long ride from here to the ranch house."

It was a standoff, and Slocum knew it. He knew as well that Dode and the other two would not follow him clear up to the ranch house. Something had to happen, and that soon. There had already been too many good cowboys killed, and Slocum did not want to see Harry get it.

"Harry," he said, "you got your gun in your hand?"

"I sure have," Harry said.

"If anything goes wrong," Slocum said, "kill them horses." He said it loud enough for Dode to hear, and then he angled his Appaloosa out away from the wagon, moving at a walk, headed straight for Dode and the other two men. Dode hauled back on his reins, and his cronies did the same.

"Slocum," he called out, "what the hell are you doing?"

"Thought I'd ride in with you," Slocum answered.

"You keep back there."

"What's wrong, Dode? There's three of you, and you're all holding rifles."

"Slocum, damn it, you come any closer, and I'll kill you."

"You'd best think about that, Dode. I'm already close enough for my Colt. Harry, can you hear me?"

"I hear you, Slocum."

"If you hear any shots, whip that team up and head for the house as fast as you can. Don't worry about me."

"Yes, sir."

"Dode, if you try anything, I'm going to kill your horses. You got me in a horse-killing mood. You can shoot me, but the three of you will be out here afoot."

"Slocum!"

"I get much closer," Slocum said, "and you'll be at a disadvantage with them rifles, won't you? You want to put them away? Go on. Put them away. I'll put my Colt away, and then we'll be even. Only thing is, there's three of you."

"You'll kill our damn horses," said Dode.

Slocum stopped riding. He threw his leg over the Appaloosa's back and slid down off the saddle. Then he slapped the big horse on the rump. "Go on, boy," he said, and the Appaloosa ran back toward the wagon. Slocum walked toward the three men. "Burl Johnson tells me I got to arrest you before I shoot," he said. "Y'all are under arrest."

Sudden panic striking him, Dode shouted, "Kill him, boys!" Slocum fired, the bullet smashing Dode's left hand against the rifle. Dode yelled and dropped the rifle, then reached for his revolver with his right hand. As soon as he fired, Slocum took a dive to his left and hit the ground rolling. Chance's and Scar's shots hit the ground behind him. When he stopped rolling, Slocum got up to one knee and fired again, hitting Chance in the belly. He fired again. This shot smashed into Scar's chest. Both men fell from their horses.

"Drop the gun, Dode," Slocum called out. Dode hesitated. He raised the gun, and Slocum fired again. Dode leaned back as the bullet tore into his chest. He looked down at the fresh wound that was pouring blood out freely. He looked at Slocum with surprise and shock written on his face, and he slumped forward in the saddle. In another minute, he slid off to one side and fell to the ground. Slocum walked over to check the bodies. They were all dead. He looked around for his horse, spotted it, and whistled. The Appaloosa came running, and Slocum mounted it and rode back over to the wagon.

"You didn't ask me for no help," Harry said.

"I'd have yelled if I got into trouble," said Slocum.

"Hell, I hope so. We going to run into any more trouble on the way to the ranch house?"

"I don't know," said Slocum. "We've got them all except for ole Mac Sowles. I think he's too much a coward to come after the two of us. Far as I know, he's all by his lonesome. He had a chance to fight me that way already, and he run off instead. Course, we'll keep our eyes peeled, but I really don't think we'll have no more trouble along the way."

"Slocum?"

"What is it, Harry?"

"Can I ask you a question?"

"Sure. Go on."

"Well, it ain't really none of my business. I know that. So if you want, just tell me to shut up my yap. But whenever I first met you, you was busting broncs for a living."

"That's right," Slocum said.

"Well, I'm just trying to figure out how you come to be so handy with that there Colt of yours."

"Ain't really no mystery, Harry," Slocum said. "I try to mind my own business, but every now and then, some son of a bitch gets in my way. I don't look for trouble, but it seems to find me."

"Like this here mess."

"Yeah."

"You coulda rode outa here, Slocum."

"I told myself that a hundred times, Harry, believe me. And maybe I should've, but people like Rance and Dode and that damn Sowles just piss me off. You know what I mean?"

Harry looked up at Slocum and smiled. "Yeah," he said. "Yeah. I know."

20

Burl Johnson was doing much better. He went back to town and was actually going to work in his office. The town fathers, though, decided to pay for two deputies at least until Johnson was back to full capacity. The poor fellow whose head had been bashed by the outlaws recovered from that ordeal. He was one of them. Both were sufficient, Johnson thought.

Slocum had ridden back over to Complacency and discovered that Sowles had shot the mayor on his way out of town, but he was greatly relieved to find out that Mayor Hager was recovering nicely from the wound and was well on course with the Circle Z case. He had talked to the judge, and they were investigating the sheriff's bank records as well of those of the Assay Office down the street. Hager assured Slocum that they had a sound case, and they were fairly sure that they had located all the loose ends. The only thing was Sowles's and the bank's money he had taken.

"Well, Mr. Mayor," Slocum said, "I could be wrong, but I believe that ole Sowles is still hanging around these parts. Like you said, he's the only one left, and he's got your bank money. He'd be smart to have cleared out, headed on down to Mexico or something, but I think he's meaner than he's smart. He wants to kill me. I think he's around all right."

• • •

Slocum was right. Sowles was around. He was up in the mountains, and he was miserable. He had his saddlebags packed with money, and he had no place to spend it. Sowles was not really an outdoorsman either. He was comfortable in a hotel room, or a restaurant, or a saloon. He liked a good steak, cooked and served by someone else. He liked good whiskey and a snuggly whore in a fine soft bed. Mexico had crossed his mind, of course, but he didn't think he would like it down there. For one thing, he couldn't speak Spanish. So he was considering San Francisco or Chicago or New York. He hadn't made up his mind.

He could ride to the nearest railroad depot, sell his horse and catch a train to one of those big cities. Once in the city, he could shave, buy a new suit of city clothes, change his name and blend right in. It was wonderful to think about. He had been thinking about it for some time. He had only been waiting for his ill-gotten gains from the Circle Z scheme to build up enough. He had made a mistake putting them in the bank, but he had wanted them to accumulate interest. He figured he would be able to make his move much sooner that way.

It had been a good plan too. It wouldn't have taken too much money. If Slocum hadn't come along, he would have been ready to move in another year, maybe less. Of course, with the proceeds from the bank robbery, he had enough money to fullfill his dream, and he was almost ready to head out. There was just one thing stopping him. Slocum. He wanted to kill Slocum before he left this wild country.

He leaned forward and picked up the coffeepot off his little campfire and poured himself another cup. Damn, but he hated this kind of lifestyle. He longed to be in comfortable surroundings. He did not like his own cooking. Not even his own coffee. What he really wanted was a good drink of whiskey. Goddamn that Slocum. He would have to kill him real soon.

Sowles considered where he would find Slocum. Slocum worked for the Circle Z Ranch. Unless Burl Johnson had

decided that the emergency was over, he also worked for
Burl. He would likely be riding back and forth between Rascality and the Circle Z. Sowles decided that he would find a
suitable spot for an ambush along the way, and he would
settle in and wait for as long as it would take. He had to also
figure out just how to do it. He wanted Slocum to know who
it was about to kill him, but he did not want to be careless
about it. Slocum was a gunfighter and a damn good one.

Sowles was going to have to find his ambush spot and
scheme up a way to let Slocum know who he was and still
get the job done. He wouldn't be able to just shoot him from
ambush, and he sure as hell wouldn't be able to face him
down. What would work? How to get Slocum sure and still
let him know? That was a real tough problem, and it would
take a lot of considering to figure it out.

Marla was riding alone into town. She rode her favorite sorrel
horse, and she wore her riding clothes. She had a saddle gun
strapped onto the side of her horse. Slocum had been out
scouting around, and her new foreman was in charge of the
ranch. She wanted to talk to the banker, so she had decided
to ride on in. There was nothing wrong with it. It had been
some time now since Dode had been killed, and the only
scoundrel left out there was that former sheriff from over at
Complacency. Marla had never even set eyes on Mac Sowles.
She was sure, though, that he was long gone. Slocum had
told her that Sowles had robbed the bank at Complacency.

She was pretty pleased with the way things had turned out.
Slocum had done her a good job. The only thing she was
not pleased about was her little assignation with Rance. It
had been fun while it lasted, but then, she hadn't known what
a bastard he was. It almost made her skin crawl to think about
what she had done with the man who almost for sure was in
on the murder of her father.

She rode around a bend in the road and was startled to see
a man sitting on horseback, blocking her path and holding a
rifle on her. He was a stocky man with a handlebar mustache.
She knew that she had never seen him before. The only thing

she could think of was that he was a highway robber. She jerked the reins back, startling her horse, but stopping it. The man sat there, the rifle trained on her, a wide smile on his face.

"What do you want?" she said. "I don't have any money on me."

"That's all right, little lady," he said. "I don't want your money."

"What then?"

"You'll find out soon enough. Slip that rifle out real careful and let it drop."

Marla did as she was told. If not money, what did the man want? She was almost afraid to think about it.

"Who are you?" she asked.

"Just stop asking questions and do what I tell you," he said. "Turn your horse around and ride to the mine."

"The mine?"

"You heard me."

Marla did what the man said. She had no choice. She rode toward the mine. Along the way, she asked again, "Who are you?" The man did not answer. "What are you going to do with me?"

"Just shut up," he said. "I'll tell you what you need to know when you need to know it."

"Mac Sowles," she said suddenly. "That's who you are."

"Well, now, ain't you the smart one? You're right. Now what good's that going to do you?"

Marla kept quiet the rest of the way to the mine. When they arrived, Sowles made her dismount and lead the way up the stairs to the office. Inside, he produced a piece of paper and a pencil.

"Now write a note," he said. "Write it to Slocum. Tell him to come out here and meet you. Tell him to come alone."

"Why should I do that?"

"Because I'll kill you if you don't, but I'll have me some fun first. You think you'd like that?" Marla made a face. "Now write."

Marla wrote: *Slocum, I'm at the mine office. I want you*

to come out here alone. I'll be waiting. Marhla.

Sowles grabbed the note away from her and read it over. "This ain't no good," he said. "Do it over. Ain't he got a first name? Make it more real." He put another piece of paper on the desk. Marla wrote again: *John, I'm waiting for you at the mine office. Please come alone. Marhla.* Sowles read the note over. It seemed all right. He laid it aside then and told her to sit in a chair. Then he took a length of rope and tied her to the chair, her hands behind her back. He checked his knots.

"That should hold you," he said. He took up the note and went outside, then down the stairs to where the horses stood waiting. He tied the note to the reins of Marla's sorrel, then tied the reins up over its neck and slapped it hard. The sorrel turned and ran. Sowles watched as the horse ran toward home. "That'll bring him," he said out loud.

Slocum had seen nothing of any interest all day long, and he decided to call it a day. But he rode toward town rather than toward the ranch house. He wanted to see how Burl Johnson was doing, and he was thinking about giving Johnson back the piece of paper that made him a deputy. He had not yet given up on finding Sowles, but he did not think that he any longer needed the deputy's commission. He was on the road headed for Rascality when he saw the rifle in the middle of the road. He stopped and dismounted to pick it up. It was a good Winchester rifle. He wondered how anyone could drop a rifle like that and not miss it. He decided to carry it on into town and leave it with Johnson. Whoever lost it might drop in to see the sheriff.

He made his way the rest of the way into town and tied his horse in front of the sheriff's office. He found Johnson inside behind the big desk. Johnson smiled broadly when Slocum walked in. He stood up and extended his hand. Slocum walked across the room and shook the hand.

"Sit back down, you ole son of a bitch," he said. "You ain't well yet."

"I'm doing pretty good though," Johnson said, "thanks to you. What brings you into town?"

"I'm just calling it a day," Slocum said. "Thought I'd come on in and see you. See how you're doing."

"No sign of that damn Sowles yet, huh?"

"No. Nothing. I've been all over too. I've about decided that he up and left the damn country."

"Likely he did," Johnson said. "He's got all that bank loot. He'd be a damn fool to hang around here. There's nothing here for him but a bullet or a noose."

"Yeah." Slocum sat on the edge of the desk and pushed his hat back. "There's just that one thing. I know damn well the son of a bitch wants to kill me real bad."

"Well, that might not be enough reason to keep him around. Like I said, he might have better sense than that."

"He might," said Slocum. He reached inside his shirt and pulled out the paper that Johnson had given him. It was rumpled. He laid it on the desk and smoothed it some. "I thought I'd give this back to you too," he said. "I really don't need it no more."

Johnson took the paper and unfolded it. He looked at it for a moment. "Why don't you keep it for a while longer?" he said. "It might come in handy."

"What for?"

"Suppose you run into Sowles after all. Suppose you kill him. This will help keep things smooth."

"You saying this here is a license to kill?"

"Well, maybe. In some cases. Go on. Stick it back in your shirt."

Slocum took it and tucked it back into his shirt. "It hangs heavy on me," he said.

"At least you're not wearing a badge. With that piece of paper, you don't have to tell anyone that you got it if you don't want to."

"I guess you're right about that. Say, you want to go over to the saloon and have a drink with me?"

"I don't know, Slocum. That's a good long walk."

"Oh, well—"

Johnson pulled open a desk drawer and brought out a bottle and two glasses, which he placed on top of the desk. "Why don't you just stay here and have one with me?"

Harry rode up to the corral to put his tired horse away for the day, and he saw the sorrel standing by the gate on the outside, still saddled. He rode up to check it. It was Miss Marla's horse all right. He reached down to open the corral gate, and he rode his own horse and led the sorrel into the corral. Then he dismounted. He unsaddled his horse. Then he turned to the sorrel. He was about to pull the saddle off when he saw the note in the bridle. He untied it, opened it and read it. Then he turned and ran to the house. He pounded on the door, but there was no answer. No one at home. It was late in the day, and there should have been someone there. He stood confused, looking around for a moment. Then he ran back to the corral, saddled another horse, and headed for town.

Slocum was on his third drink when Harry burst through the front door of the sheriff's office. Slocum and Johnson were both surprised by the abrupt entrance. "Harry, what—"

"Here," said Harry, holding the note out toward Slocum. Slocum took it and read it.

"Well, it's kinda strange," he said. "Where'd you get it?"

Harry told Slocum about finding the sorrel outside the corral still saddled. "I was sure glad I seen your horse out there," he added.

"Yeah," said Slocum. "Me too. Say, how do you spell Marla?"

"M-a-r-l-a," said Johnson. "Why?"

"Look at this." Slocum handed the note to Johnson.

"That's peculiar," Johnson said.

"In the first place," said Harry, "if she was really wanting to meet you at the mine, how come her horse come to the ranch all by itself?"

"That's one good question," said Slocum. "Another one is how come her to spell her name this way?"

"Harry, did you look for Marla at the house?" Slocum asked.

"Hell yes, Slocum."

"Slocum, this don't look good," said Johnson.

"I'm going out to the mine," said Slocum.

"I'll go with you," said Harry.

"No, you don't," Slocum said. "The note says alone. I don't want no one going with me."

"What is it, Slocum?" Harry asked.

"It looks to me like someone's got her, Harry. That's how come she spelled her name funny, and that's how come her horse showed up alone at the ranch. If someone's got her out there, you know they can see all over hell from that office. I can't have anyone come along with me."

"But, Slocum—"

"Never mind, Harry," Johnson said. "Slocum's right. Go on, Slocum. Get out of here. And good luck."

Slocum ran out the door. Harry looked after him for a moment, then looked back at Johnson.

"We'll follow him, Harry. Don't worry. We'll stay far enough back that no one'll see us, but if we hear any gunshots, we'll move up quick. Get us a couple of horses, will you?"

Slocum had a time holding back his Appaloosa. He wanted to rush on out to the mine. It had to be Sowles, the son of a bitch. He was afraid to face Slocum, so he had grabbed Marla and used her to get Slocum to the mine alone. Slocum knew what he was up to. If he had Marla in the mine office, he would have a good shot at Slocum. And as long as he had Marla, he could tell Slocum what to do and Slocum wouldn't be able to argue with him. He would have to do it.

He slowed his pace. He had to think. What would he do? Stand down there and let Sowles blow his guts out? What would Sowles do to Marla then? It didn't make sense. He couldn't just ignore it. He had to do something, but just riding out to the mine the way Sowles wanted him to was not the way. There had to be a better way. There had to be a way to get to the man before he was able to do anything to Marla. Then it came to him, and he turned his horse around and headed back to town. Along the way, he met Harry and Johnson.

"What the hell are you doing?" he said. "I told you not to follow me."

"We were hanging way back," said Harry.

"Burl, you shouldn't even be out riding like this."

"I'm all right, Slocum, but tell me, what were you doing headed back for town?"

"I got me an idea, Burl, and I need your help. Well, I really need Harry's help. Tell you what. Let's sit down and work this thing out together."

They sat and talked for a while. Then Slocum and Harry traded shirts, hats, and horses. It took some talking from Slocum, but the big Appaloosa at last let Harry ride. Johnson stayed where he was and built a small campfire. He would wait there. Harry mounted up and rode straight for the mine, and Slocum rode south toward the mountains. He did not really know just where he was going, but he knew there had to be a way. He was only afraid that Harry would reach the mine office too early.

Arriving at the foot of the mountains, Slocum found no place he could go up with a horse. He turned to ride north along the edge of the rise as close as he could get to the mine without being seen. In a while, he had to abandon his horse. He looked up the side of the mountain until he found a way, and then he started to climb. Slocum was in a hurry, but he had to be careful. He could not really hurry up this mountain. If he slipped and fell, no one would be helped. He moved carefully, searching for hand- and footholds in the dark.

Once his foot slipped, and he wound up hanging by his fingers. He felt around with both feet until one foot managed to plant itself on something solid. He took a deep breath and again began crawling up the steep side of the treacherous mountain. At last he found a ledge, and he started walking along it, hoping that he was high enough to be above the mine office. He thought he was, but he really wouldn't know until he got there.

Harry rode up to just beyond rifle range of the mine office on the side of the mountain and stopped. There was a bright moon in the sky, and he knew that he could be seen. He sat there for a moment, wondering where Slocum was and how he was doing. He didn't really want to be seen too soon. He tried to find some sign of Slocum on the side of the mountain, but he couldn't see anything up there. Someone saw him though.

"Slocum? That you?"

"Yeah," Harry called back.

"I've got Marla up here."

"Yeah."

"You know who I am, don't you?"

"I know. Sowles."

"Come on in closer."

Harry urged the Appaloosa a little closer.

"What's wrong, Slocum? I ain't going to shoot you like this. Come on closer."

Harry moved closer still, but Sowles hollered at him to stop. "That's close enough. Take off your gun belt and drop it." Harry unbuckled the belt and dropped it on the ground. "Now the Winchester." Harry dragged the rifle out of the scabbard and tossed it aside. "Now you can come on up," said Sowles. As Harry moved closer, Sowles stepped out onto the landing in front of the office. "I want you to be able to see me, Slocum. I want you to know who it is that's about to kill you. I want you to think about it and remember why."

Harry rode the Appaloosa a little closer. He was keeping his head down to avoid being recognized. "Look up here, Slocum," Sowles shouted. "Didn't you hear me? I said I want you to see me. Look up."

Harry lifted his head, hoping that the darkness would still cloud his features enough that Sowles would be fooled, but Sowles was not. He was confused.

"Hey," he said. "What is this? What's wrong? Come here.

Come on up here." Harry rode up closer. "Get off that horse and come up these stairs," said Sowles. Harry dismounted slowly and walked toward the stairs. Damn, he thought, where is that Slocum? "Come on. Come on," said Sowles. Harry stepped on the first step, then the second. He was about halfway up the stairs before Sowles stopped him again. "Look up here at me," Sowles demanded. Harry looked up. "You ain't Slocum. Where the hell is Slocum? What are you trying to pull on me?" The next voice came from behind and above him.

"Sowles, drop the gun."

Sowles whirled fast and fired a wild shot up toward the roof of the mine office, and then Slocum fired one shot. The bullet tore into Sowles's forehead, and as he fell back off the landing, he was dead. The body hit halfway down to the ground with a sickening thud, and then it slid the rest of the way.

"Slocum," said Harry. "Damn, I'm glad to see you."

"Get inside and see if Marla's in there," Slocum said.

Harry ran the rest of the way up the stairs and crashed through the door while Slocum backed off the roof to hang by the eaves and drop to the landing. He hurried inside after Harry, who almost had the ropes off of Marla.

"You all right, Marla?" Slocum said.

"I'm all right," she said. "How did you—"

"Never mind that just now," Slocum said. "Let's get out of here."

The three of them rode back to the small camp where Burl Johnson was waiting anxiously. Slocum and Harry had to tell the whole tale of how they confused Sowles, and how Slocum killed him. Then Johnson produced his bottle from behind him.

"I didn't bring along any glasses, but I'll be glad to pass this around," he said.

"I'll take a snort," said Harry.

"Ladies first," said Johnson, offering the bottle to Marla.

She took it, smiled at Burl Johnson, and said, "Thanks, Burl. This is just what I need."

Watch for

SLOCUM AND THE DEADLY DAMSEL

294th novel in the exciting SLOCUM series
from Jove

Coming in August!